ROYALLY UNEXPECTED

LAURA ASHWOOD

ANCHORED SOUL PUBLISHING

This book is a work of fiction. The names, characters, places, and incidents are all products of the author's imagination and are not to be construed as real. Any resemblances to persons, organizations, events, or locales are entirely coincidental.

Royally Unexpected
Copyright © 2022 by Laura Ashwood

All rights reserved. The book contains material protected under International and Federal Copyright Laws and Treaties. No part of this book may be reproduced or transmitted in any form or by any means, electronic or mechanical, including photocopying, recording, or by any information storage system without express written permission from the author.

To request permission, contact anchoredsoulpublishing@gmail.com.

This book is licensed for your personal enjoyment only. This book may not be re-sold or given away to other people. If you would like to share this book with another person, please purchase an additional copy for each recipient. If you're reading this book and did not purchase it, or it was not purchased for your use only, then please return and purchase your own copy. Thank you for respecting the hard work of this author.

Scriptures quoted from the King James Holy Bible.

Cover Design by EDH Graphics

GET FREE BOOKS!

You're just a away from:

* A FREE book
* VIP notice of sales and freebies
* Author happenings
* Great recipes
* Exclusive giveaways
* Special bonus content
* First peek at new covers and titles

Just scan the QR code to sign up for Laura's newsletter, or visit www.lauraashwood.com!

To every thing there is a season, and a time to every purpose under the heaven.

~ Ecclesiastes 3: 1

CONTENTS

Chapter 1	1
Chapter 2	23
Chapter 3	43
Chapter 4	63
Chapter 5	79
Chapter 6	99
Chapter 7	113
Chapter 8	129
Chapter 9	145
Chapter 10	161
Chapter 11	183
Chapter 12	197
Chapter 13	213

Chapter 14	229
Chapter 15	247
Chapter 16	267
Chapter 17	283
Chapter 18	301
Chapter 19	323
Chapter 20	343
Epilogue	351
About Laura	359

CHAPTER 1

There had to be more to life than this.

The roar from the cannons was deafening. Prince Dorian Tennesley let out a long sigh and tried not to fidget as he stood at attention for the royal salute. Once the cannons were quiet, his mother, Queen Sophia, reigning monarch of Avington, waved to her subjects. The park in central Avington was filled with men, women and children, and Dorian's eye twitched as the crowd erupted with cheers and applause.

What did people find so entertaining about seeing his family? Dorian never understood the fascination. He couldn't remember a time he wasn't being hounded by fans or paparazzi. To him, it was all pomp and circumstance, and he was tired of it. As the second son, and fourth in line to the throne, it wasn't like his appearance there mattered. But his mother insisted. "It's your duty," she'd admonished when he'd told her he wasn't interested. *Duty, obligation, responsibility.* It didn't matter which word she used, it all amounted to the same thing—a life that wasn't his own.

Today's ceremony was to honor the President of Ireland's arrival in the small island country of Avington, and marked the third such visit in as many months. The sun shone brightly, and a cool breeze floated in off the sea, ruffling a wisp of hair off his forehead. Dorian's mind wandered as the queen introduced the visiting president.

Dorian scanned the crowd and settled his gaze on a pretty woman standing next to a large hawthorn tree. She stared back at him and shot him a seductive grin. His eyebrows twitched, and he fought to keep his expression neutral. She raised a slender arm and wiggled her fingers at him before pressing them to her cherry red lips and blowing him a kiss. Someone softly cleared their throat next to him, and Dorian suppressed a groan. *Philip.* He slid a glance to the right and met his older brother's icy glare. Before Dorian could react, the throng of onlookers broke into a roar of applause and Philip turned to follow the queen toward the waiting carriages that would take them through town and back to the castle.

Dorian's gaze flicked back to the hawthorn tree, but the woman was no longer there. Heaving a sigh, he turned and proceeded toward the rest of their entourage. The royal carriages were made of fine wood, their panels painted in forest green with carved wood and gilt moldings. The doors were emblazoned with the Avington royal arms. Ornamental brass and crystal lamps adorned the four corners of each carriage's body, and they were upholstered in fine chestnut leather. The hoods were folded back, and two uniformed footmen sat in each rumble. A postilion guided each team of black Friesian horses.

The queen paused and gave the crowd a final wave before climbing into the first of two horse-drawn carriages, alongside the visiting president and his wife. Dorian climbed into the second carriage with his brother Philip, Philip's wife Anna, and his one-year-old nephew Archer. Archer squealed and pointed at the horses, and some of the tension left Dorian's shoulders as he smiled at the youngster. He loved his nephew, loved kids really, but wasn't sure he saw them in his future. Kids meant marriage. Dorian shuddered at the thought.

Mounted soldiers from the Avington Cavalry escorted the two carriages out of Battenburg Park and they wound their way through the streets of Avington toward Dorburn Castle. Brightly colored Avington flags adorned the light poles, and people lined the road to the castle hoping to catch a glimpse of the royal family. Archer sat on Anna's lap happily blowing spit bubbles. Dorian couldn't help chuckling at the contented little boy.

Dorian admired Anna for insisting that Archer come along with the family to public events. When he and Philip were young, they were relegated to the care of one of the many nannies that came and went. At least in some ways, times had changed.

As they drove through the city, Philip and Anna waved and smiled, while Dorian drummed his fingers along the top of the door frame, counting the minutes until they arrived at the castle, and he could get away.

"You just can't help yourself, can you?" Philip asked in a harsh whisper once the horses were past the gates, and they were away from the watchful gazes of the crowds.

Dorian narrowed his gaze at his brother. "What are you talking about?"

Philip rolled his eyes. "The girl. In the crowd. I saw you making eyes at her. Are you trying to get more bad press?"

Dorian's lips curled into a smirk as he recalled the kiss the pretty brunette had blown him. "Are you jealous, brother?"

Anna shot him a look that clearly said, *You're a moron,* then turned back to Archer, her lips pressed into a thin line. Dorian lifted an indifferent shoulder and shifted his gaze back to Philip, who let out a snort.

"I have higher standards than that, *brother*," Philip retorted. "You know as well as I do that the media is watching you like a hawk right now. They aren't going to have missed that exchange."

Dorian grinned. "It's not my fault women find me irresistible."

"Have fun explaining that to Mother when it's tomorrow's headline."

The grin slipped from Dorian's face. While being part of a royal family had always made them of interest to the press, it seemed that lately he'd become their target. No matter what he did, the paparazzi were there spinning their own version of things. *Or someone else's version.* Whatever version sold the most, regardless of whether it was true or not. Tension climbed Dorian's spine and the muscles in his shoulders tightened.

"Whatever," he snapped at Philip. "You don't know what it's like."

"You're right. I don't," Philip conceded. "But I don't go out of my way to attract negative attention either."

Dorian held his brother's icy glare. "Not all of us were born perfect," he ground out.

Philip's retort was cut off by Anna's motion for silence as the carriages rolled to a stop in front of Dorburn Castle. Dorian shot his brother one last glare before disembarking and joining the rest of the entourage at the entrance to the castle. He stole a quick glance at his watch and released an annoyed sigh. Because the ceremony at the park had run long, he would no longer have time to visit Gatsby before his *required* presence at the state banquet.

Just get through this night and you're done playing Prince for the rest of the summer, he told himself as he pasted a smile on his face and followed the group through the gatehouse and into the great hall. The rest of the group mingled while Dorian stood off to the side and waited. *Three months with no obligations.* He wasn't sure what he was going to do with his time off from royal duties, but he knew it wouldn't be spent in Avington. Anywhere but here. Somewhere far away from his condescending brother and disappointed mother. He began making a mental list of places he'd like to visit when a soft touch on his arm interrupted his thoughts. He turned, and his eyebrows lifted in mild surprise as he met his mother's gaze.

"Is something troubling you, son?" she asked.

Dorian thought he caught a flicker of concern in her cool blue eyes for just a moment before she glanced around the room, smiling at her guests. His stomach tightened. *Of course, she was concerned. Concerned that he wasn't doing his part.*

"You know I don't like these events, Mother."

Her gaze held his for what seemed like an eternity, the expression on her face unreadable. Dorian refused to look away. He was tired of being forced to take part in all of these formal events where his presence wasn't necessary. Was he acting like a spoiled child? Perhaps, but at this point, he didn't much care. He just wanted the day to be done so he could get on with what he wanted to do, even though he had no idea what that might be.

"I would like to speak with you privately after the banquet," she finally said, her lips curving back into the practiced smile she wore in public.

Dorian stifled a groan but nodded. Satisfied with his response, his mother turned and signaled to the butler that she was ready.

Dorian took his place behind his brother and sister-in-law for the royal procession into the ballroom for the state banquet. He closed his eyes and silently cursed when he saw he'd been paired once again with Ingrid Pelham, Countess of Domhnall. *How had he not seen her earlier? How had she not seen him was the bigger question.* His mother insisted on putting them together at every available opportunity. He was certain it wasn't by chance.

He steeled himself, greeted Ingrid with a forced smile and offered her his elbow, as was his duty. She gripped it like a piranha attacking its prey.

"Dorian," she gushed as she peered up at him through long, dark eyelashes that he was sure were glued onto her eyelids. "I've been looking everywhere for you." She glanced around as though looking to make sure they were alone, then said, "I heard all about your break-up with Candace Easton. You poor thing." She placed her hand on his arm and gave it a light squeeze.

Dorian narrowed his eyes at her honeyed tone, and carefully removed her hand from his arm. *I'm sure you have.* She had made it no secret that she intended to become the next princess of Avington. "Lady Ingrid," he replied curtly and focused his attention forward. He hated to be rude, but he wasn't in the mood to deal with her overt advances.

"Aren't you going to tell me how good I look?" Ingrid turned to the side and batted her eyelashes at him from over her bare shoulder.

Dorian studied her for a moment. She was waif-thin, which was accentuated by the tight-fitting black gown she wore. The black was in stark contrast to her chin-length straight blonde hair. Her wide, cat-like eyes were heavily made up in dark shadow, and sparkly pink makeup accentuated her cheekbones. Dark lipstick lined her heart-shaped lips.

He supposed some men might think she was beautiful. Until she opened her mouth, that is. Just like Candace. Candace was dark to Ingrid's blonde, but wore her makeup in the same dramatic fashion. He wondered if either one of them would be recognizable without it. In his mind, they relied too much on surface glamor and failed to understand that a woman's true beauty came from within.

Dorian forced a smile. "You look lovely, as always." Ingrid beamed, clearly failing to hear the slight sarcasm in his voice. Thankfully, the line moved, and the procession entered the grand ballroom where the enormous mahogany table had been set for the 150 or so guests who had been invited based upon their cultural or diplomatic links to Avington and Ireland.

Several of the guests, including Ingrid and her family, were regular invitees. Dorian and Ingrid were seated next to one another near the head of the table, and he fought the urge to trade places with the gentleman next to him.

Once all the guests were situated, Queen Sophia stood and welcomed everyone. With her long, dark brown hair swept into a chignon at the nape of her neck and an emerald tiara atop her head, the queen was a stunning woman. Despite his annoyance with her, Dorian admired his mother. She had taken the crown at a young age, after a short illness took the life of her father, King Edward. Dorian had never had the opportunity to meet his grandfather, but he knew he was a well-loved man that ruled his country with wisdom and justice. His mother followed his example and was revered and respected by not only the citizens of Avington, but by leaders of the neighboring European countries as well.

The queen delivered her welcome speech. Dorian listened for a few moments but found his mind wandering once again to possible vacation destinations. He'd already decided to take this trip solo. Maybe he'd spend a little time thinking about what he wanted to do with his life. His mother had been pressuring him a lot more lately to work in an official capacity. He had no desire to ride his brother's coattails and had no interest in being a foreign diplomat.

A round of polite applause brought Dorian out of his reverie, and the guests visited amongst themselves as the staff brought in the meal. Ingrid wasted no time in continuing her flirtation.

"I'm quite put out that you never called." She pursed her painted pink lips together in a pout.

Dorian gritted his teeth. *What was she talking about?* "I don't recall that I was supposed to."

"Well, now that you're single again, there's no reason for us--"

"Us? What are you talking about?" Dorian hissed. He glanced quickly around to see if anyone was listening to them. Everyone appeared to be engaged in their own conversations and he felt a small measure of relief. The last thing he needed, or wanted, was to be romantically linked with her.

"What?" Ingrid widened her eyes in mock innocence and blinked at him. "We're perfect for each other." Her lips curled into a sly smile. "You know, I could help you get over her."

Was she trying to be sympathetic? If so, it wasn't working. Not to mention he didn't think Ingrid possessed a single gram of genuine sympathy for anything that didn't serve some benefit to her. Dorian swallowed hard and forced down his temper.

He had met Candace Easton while he was in the French Riviera with his friends on holiday. She was an American actress that was there on location for a film she was starring in. He'd been captivated by her beauty and charm. They'd quickly become darlings in the media and their relationship was highly publicized.

It hadn't taken very long for Dorian to realize they had absolutely nothing in common. The entire basis of her attraction to him was his title and what it could do for her acting career. When he'd broken things off just a few short weeks ago, she'd gone ballistic. She began spreading lies about him on every social media outlet she could. Even worse, she partook in countless entertainment television interviews so she could tell *her* side of the story. And her side of the story was nothing close to reality.

That was bad enough, but now Ingrid was trying to use that debacle to position herself closer to him. She wasn't any better than Candace had been. He'd given up on finding someone that would love him for him, and not just because of his title.

Dorian stared at her for a long moment and with a deliberate movement, lifted her hand off his arm. "Ingrid, that's enough," he said, lowering his voice to a barely audible level. "I've warned you before that you and I are not going to happen. You need to stop this nonsense."

She sniffed. "We'll just see about that."

They managed to make it through the rest of the meal without further incident or comment. After the plates were cleared and the guests dismissed, Dorian headed toward the other end of the castle and approached his mother's study. He couldn't imagine what it was that she wanted to talk to him about, but for some reason he had a feeling that his vacation was about to be taken off the table. He knocked lightly and pushed the door open without waiting for a response.

Dorian stopped short when he saw that Philip occupied one of the two chairs positioned on the other side of the ornate oak desk where his mother sat. Philip glanced at him from over the rim of a teacup and grinned like a cat who'd just swallowed a canary. *Of course, Philip would be involved with whatever grand plan his mother wanted to discuss with him.*

His mother smiled at him as he entered the room. "Dorian, please have a seat." She gestured toward the empty chair next to Philip. Dorian clenched his jaw so hard he thought he might crack a molar, but complied.

"I would like to discuss your royal duties. I feel as though you've been...floundering a bit since your retirement from the Army," she said.

Duties. Dorian bristled at the word. His whole life was structured around fulfilling his royal duties. He was always surrounded by an entourage of people making sure he followed their carefully orchestrated plans, their itinerary. The few times he'd dared to go off on his own, he'd fallen under the media's unforgiving microscope. He knew he was seen as little more than a disappointment to his mother since his return a year ago from his stint in the Avington Army.

The truth was, Dorian missed being in the military. He liked the structure and sense of purpose it gave him. He'd felt as though he was actually doing something worthwhile while he was enlisted but, as a member of the royal family, he was forced to retire after ten years of service.

Now, he didn't know what to do with his time. It wasn't like he could just go out and get a job. Since the birth of his nephew, and with another niece or nephew on the way, there was little to no chance he'd ever take the throne, not that he wanted to. Philip had been groomed for the crown since the day he was born, and Dorian was happy to let him have the honor, even though his older brother liked to hold it above him on a regular basis.

"I've made arrangements for you to embark on a goodwill tour of the United States," his mother continued. She slid a sheet of paper across her desk toward him. "This is the itinerary. You'll have to meet with security and the press secretary, of course."

Dorian straightened in his chair and his stomach churned as he glanced at the list of appearances he'd be required to make. *Was she serious?* He never made public appearances on behalf of Avington. That duty had always been relegated to Philip. He lifted his gaze to meet hers and his forehead wrinkled.

"You want *me* to go?"

His mother glanced at Philip then back to Dorian. "We thought it might be a good opportunity for you."

We? Dorian's fingers tightened on the arms of the chair. *Of course, his brother had something to do with this plan.* He knew how much Dorian disliked being put on display. Dorian had been looking forward to having some time alone, away, to think. Not to play "prince".

"Why not Philip?" Dorian argued. "He's better at these kinds of things than I am." The words tasted sour coming out of his mouth, but it was true. Philip had a way of making people like him in an instant, no matter where he went. It wasn't like that for Dorian.

"Don't you think it's time you start contributing?" Philip placed his teacup on the desk and stared at Dorian.

A surge of anger shot through Dorian, and he shoved his chair away from the desk. *He didn't need this.*

"That's enough!" His mother slapped her palm on the surface of the desk.

Dorian froze and the two brothers exchanged a guilty glance. Their mother never raised her voice.

She gave them each a pointed glare, then settled her gaze on Dorian and folded her hands on the table. "Quite frankly, Dorian, you need to improve your public image. This will give you an opportunity to do that, as well as boost Avington's relations with the United States."

Dorian's mouth went dry and his cheeks burned with shame. She was right. He hated that she was right, but she was. "None of what's been said about me is true," he said in a resigned tone.

His mother's mouth tightened. "Nevertheless, it has not been good publicity for Avington. This will give you a chance to show yourself, and Avington, in a positive light."

"If he doesn't screw it up," Philip chortled.

Dorian pressed his lips together. His mother had a point. This would be a good way to improve his reputation. It might not be the vacation he'd had in mind, but maybe this was what he needed. A chance to prove himself. A chance to prove Philip wrong. He sat straighter in the chair and grinned as a lightness filled him. A lightness he'd never felt before.

"Let's do this."

CHAPTER 2

EMMIE WALKER WAS ON top of the world. She and Bernie, aka Royce's Royal Achy Breaky Heart, had just won Best in Show at the prestigious Crestwood Hills Dog Show in New York City. It was Bernie's last show, and she was giddy that he was retiring on top. Plus, the win here would go a long way toward cementing her credibility as a trainer and handler. *One step closer.*

The tricolor Cardigan Welsh Corgi gazed up at her with his deep brown eyes, and Emmie swore he was smiling at her. She'd been working with him for several years and would miss the saucy little dog.

She heard her name being called and turned to see Royce Anderson, Bernie's owner, making his way through the crowd toward her. He was accompanied by an older gentleman whom Emmie didn't recognize.

"Way to go out in style, old man!" Royce beamed, crouching to ruffle the fur of the happy corgi's head. He stood and turned to Emmie. "Congratulations to you too," he said, offering his hand. "There will be a hefty bonus in your final check. You've really done us proud."

Emmie shook his hand and gave him a grateful smile. "Thank you, Mr. Anderson. Bernie was in fine form today."

Royce nodded in agreement and gestured to the gentlemen next to him. "Emmie, I'd like you to meet Montgomery Harrison. Montgomery, this is the wonder woman I was telling you about, Emmeline Walker."

Mr. Harrison extended his hand. "Miss Walker, it's a pleasure."

Emmie cheeks grew warm at the unexpected compliment from Royce. She met Mr. Harrison's gaze, grasped his hand in a firm handshake, and gave a slight nod of her head.

"Montgomery is a dear friend of mine and he's looking for a short-term handler," Royce continued. "It's a great opportunity and I thought you might be interested. I'm going to leave you two to talk so I can schmooze with the media." He chuckled, picked up Bernie, said goodbye to Mr. Harrison, and strode away.

Emmie assessed the gentleman in front of her. He wore a finely tailored black suit with a dove-grey vest. A matching dove-grey top hat was tucked under his arm. The neatly trimmed dark hair on the sides of his head was liberally streaked with grey, and he was bald on top. He sported a very well-groomed salt and pepper mustache and goatee under a strong nose. There was an almost....regal look about him. *What could someone like him possibly want with her?*

"Miss Walker," Mr. Harrison began, "I have a business proposal I'd like to discuss with you."

Business proposal? Emmie wasn't really in the mood to listen to this man's spiel, but Royce had been good to her, and she felt she owed it to him to at least hear what Mr. Harrison had to say. She crossed her arms over her chest and hoped he would be quick about it. "Go on," she said.

"I am in need of an experienced dog handler to accompany a dignitary and his dog while he conducts a goodwill tour of the United States."

A dignitary? Goodwill tour? Emmie stifled a giggle. *Did he think she was that naive? What kind of joke was Royce playing?*

Mr. Harrison continued, oblivious to the commentary playing out in Emmie's mind. "Your job would be the exclusive care and handling of his dog while he is traveling. All your expenses would be covered, of course."

"Of course," Emmie chuckled and shook her head. *This had gone on long enough.* She needed to get Bernie's equipment packed up so she could head home. Her grandmother hadn't been feeling well and she was anxious to return so she could care for her. "Look, Mr. Harrison, if this is some sort of joke between you and Mr. Anderson, it's in poor taste and I don't have time for it." She turned and collected Bernie's things.

"I assure you Miss Walker, this is no joke," Mr. Harrison said.

There was a note of urgency in his voice that hadn't been there before, and Emmie hesitated. *Could this be for real?* She turned and faced the older gentleman again.

He continued. "For security reasons, I am unable to divulge detailed information until contracts have been signed, but I have known Mr. Anderson for many years, and I think you'll find he will be more than happy to vouch for my character, as well as that of my employer."

Emmie placed a hand on her hip, lifted her chin and set her gaze on him. "Why me? Surely, a dignitary would have his own trainer and staff. I'm just a nobody." *And after today, an unemployed nobody.* "I'm not even credentialed."

"You come very highly recommended by a trusted friend. His Ro– uh, my employer does have a trainer on staff. However, he has taken ill and is unable to travel. So, as you can see, we are in quite a bind."

Emmie considered that. She'd been working in the show dog world for a number of years and knew most of the top owners wouldn't travel without a trainer for their dogs, especially in the weeks prior to a show.

"When is this...goodwill trip, or whatever it's called?"

Mr. Harrison pulled an envelope from his inside coat pocket and handed it to her. "I have taken the liberty of drawing up a contract for you to review. It includes calendar and compensation details."

She took the envelope and ran her finger along the flap but didn't open it. She'd known and worked for Mr. Anderson for a number of years and had grown to trust and respect the man. *Surely, he wouldn't recommend someone to her that wasn't trustworthy, would he?* She closed her eyes for a moment and tried to think what her Nana would say.

Emmie had come to live with her grandmother after her parents died and left her an orphan. A shy child by nature, she'd withdrawn even more after the tragedy, and her grandmother encouraged her to get involved with showing dogs to bring her out of her shell. It had been a natural fit and she'd worked with dogs, in one capacity or another, ever since.

Her dream was to one day own her own training facility, and she'd been scrimping and saving for years. However, with her grandmother's failing health and mounting medical bills, and with Emmie the only one to help, that dream seemed farther and farther away every day.

"You would need to be ready to leave by the end of the week in order to process your credentials and prepare you for the tour," Mr. Harrison continued.

Emmie's head snapped up. She needed to go back to Minnesota to see Nana. "That's too soon."

Mr. Harrison held up his hand. "I understand it's short notice. Mr. Anderson assured me you were through with your assignment to him, and you'll be handsomely compensated for your inconvenience." He reached inside his coat again, pulled out a business card and pressed it into her hand. "I realize you may need some time to think about it. Please review the information I've given you. Feel free to speak with Mr. Anderson, if you'd like, then call me at the number on the card with your decision. I'll be in town through tomorrow." He gave a nod of his head, then turned and disappeared into the crowd.

"Okay, thank you," she replied, but he was already gone. Emmie flipped the card over. It was heavy, slightly textured paper with silver edging. An unfamiliar decorative crest was embossed in the upper left corner along with lettering that read *Montgomery Harrison, Private Secretary*. A phone number with an overseas country code was printed below the name, and a handwritten local number was scrawled beneath.

Private Secretary. Emmie stared at the card for a long moment, then shoved it, along with the envelope inside her bag to deal with later. Right now, she needed to get her show case packed, along with Bernie's things for Mr. Anderson before he returned. While she gathered her things, her mind replayed the conversation with Mr. Harrison. She'd met a fair number of celebrities in her years working with show dogs, but couldn't recall anyone that would use the title of dignitary.

Her thoughts were interrupted by the familiar chirp of her cell phone, and Emmie dug through her bag to pull it out. She recognized the number as the business office of the assisted living center where her grandmother lived. Grimacing, she pressed the button to decline the call. She closed her eyes and took a deep breath as a wave of guilt washed over her. She was a few days late with her grandmother's rent payment. She'd be able to pay it with the earnings from this event, and hopefully another month or two in advance with whatever bonus she got from Mr. Anderson. *But what happens after that?*

The corner of the envelope Mr. Harrison had given her caught her eye. *You'll be handsomely compensated for your inconvenience,* he'd said. Curiosity got the better of her and she pulled the envelope back out of her bag and slid her finger along the edge of the flap. She removed the papers and one by one, she pored over the sheets of information.

The job seemed pretty straightforward. She would be charged with the care and handling of a corgi, and in exchange would be provided with a private room, a travel wardrobe, and all travel and meal expenses while on the tour. *A travel wardrobe?* Emmie glanced down at the plain black skirt, white blouse, and sensible shoes she wore and shrugged. She'd never been much of one to chase the latest fashion trends, especially when those clothes generally only looked good on people who were less...full figured. Not to mention how much stylish clothing cost. Most of her clothes came from the clearance rack at the department store. *A new wardrobe might be fun.*

She flipped the page where the compensation package was set out and nearly dropped it, doing a double take when she saw the amount she would be paid for the job. It was more than she normally made in a year for what amounted to a month's worth of time. She'd be able to catch up her grandmother's rent and maybe even upgrade her rickety old late model car with something more reliable. Still, she hesitated. It was one thing to be gone for a few days here and there, but this would take her away from her grandmother for over a month. Who would make sure she was okay?

Don't look a gift horse in the mouth, Emmie-, Nana's words echoed in her head as her phone chirped again. An odd tingle ran down Emmie's spine as Nana's name appeared on the screen. It wasn't unusual for her grandmother to call her when she was traveling, but she normally didn't call when she knew Emmie was at a show. She ignored the slight twist in her stomach and swiped the screen to answer. "Hi Nana, is everything okay?"

"Is this Emmeline Walker?" An unfamiliar voice came across the line. Emmie's stomach completed the twist and was now doing flip flops. *Had something happened to Nana? Please no, not now. God, please let her be all right*, she prayed.

"Yes, who is this?" she said into the phone. "Where's Blanche?" Emmie tried to keep the panic from her voice. Her grandmother hadn't been feeling well for some time now, and the doctors hadn't been able to make heads nor tails of her symptoms. She'd seemed fine a few days ago when Emmie had left, but as she knew all too well, things could change in an instant. Her vision blurred and she held her breath while she waited for a reply.

"Honey, this is Agnes, I'm Blanche's neighbor. We met at the knitting group a few weeks ago. You remember, I was making that blanket that ended up being a washcloth because I had to keep tearing out stitches and Blanche told me I was better off starting small?" The older woman chuckled.

Emmie remembered. Agnes was not the kind of woman you easily forgot. She was a portly woman with a penchant for wearing tight floral dresses and a bright pink faux fur shoulder wrap, no matter what the season. She'd recently joined the knitting group Nana belonged to, and well, to say she was struggling was being kind.

"Yes, I remember you, Agnes. Where's Nana?" Emmie repeated.

"Well, you know we have bridge club today. I went over to Blanche's apartment so we could walk together, but she didn't answer the door. It's not like her not to wait for me, but I was running a little late and thought maybe she just went to the community room without me. But when I got there, she wasn't there either. So, I called—"

"Agnes, what happened? Where is Nana?" Emmie interrupted, now unable to hide the panic in her voice.

"Honey, she's in the hospital."

Emmie reached for the folding chair next to the table at her portable grooming station and sank into it. "W-what happened? Is she okay?"

"They say she's a little dehydrated. She asked me to call you instead of having one of the snooty nurses call. That fancy new doctor from the city is with her right now and he's running all kinds of tests." Agnes paused, then added in a conspiratorial tone, "She's giving him a piece of her mind about it too."

Emmie blew out a tense breath and tried to relax. Blanche hated doctors and it didn't surprise her one bit that she would have made Agnes call her rather than have one of the hospital staff do it, or that she was giving the doctor a hard time. Emmie had been fighting her for weeks to have more tests run, but she had refused. She tried to be optimistic. Maybe the new doctor would find something the others had missed.

Agnes continued. "They're going to keep her for a spell. She got herself all worked up, so they gave her a little something to settle her down. I think you kids call it a chill pill."

Emmie sighed and rubbed her temples. "Can I talk to her?"

"The doctor is just leaving so I'll put her on. I hope you had a nice time at your little dog show and tell."

Emmie closed her eyes and counted to three before she spoke, "Thank you Agnes."

There was a muffled conversation on the other end of the phone and then Emmie heard her grandmother's voice, a little softer and slower than usual. "Emmie, how did your show go?"

It was just like her to be concerned about what Emmie was doing over her own needs. "We won Best in Show, Nana, but that's not important. What's going on with you? Are you okay?"

"That newfangled doctor has all kinds of ideas. He's going to make me stay here for a few days. Wants to run every dang-blasted test there is. Use me as a pincushion."

"I'm sure he just wants to be thorough, Nana. Maybe he'll be able to tell you why you're so tired all the time."

Emmie could almost feel Nana's ragged breaths through the phone.

"Em, he thinks I've got the cancer," Nana said. She sounded tired and resigned.

Emmie inhaled sharply, covered her mouth with her hand while her stomach plummeted to the floor. *No! She's all the family I have left.* While she knew her grandmother wouldn't live forever, of course, she wasn't ready to lose her just yet. Her vision blurred and she tried to steady her voice. "C-cancer? Are they sure? Where?" Emmie had a million questions and didn't know where to start asking them.

"He said there's some suspicious spots in my lungs. They want to take pictures of it. Can you imagine? He said I have to meet with some sort of specialist, a gyno-onco-ologist. I told him I haven't had no need for that kind of doctor for a long time but he insisted. I don't know what they think an old lady needs to see one of those doctors for."

The corners of Emmie's mouth turned up despite the gravity of the news. "They want you to meet with an oncologist, Nana, not a gynecologist. An oncologist is a–a cancer doctor."

Her grandma sniffed. "Well, either way, I don't want to see one. I told them my insurance wouldn't pay for that kind of nonsense, but he won't listen to me."

Emmie's heart sank. She didn't think lung cancer had a very good prognosis, but it would explain the lingering cough Nana had had. The medical bills would be astronomical for her grandmother who was on a fixed income. Her stomach twisted. *How was she going to come up with the money to help with the medical bills*? Emmie pulled out Mr. Harrison's business card and stared at it.

"Nana, don't you worry one bit about the bills. I got a new job offer today and I'll help. You just listen to your new doctor and get better."

"Em, you are a good girl. You just do your job and don't fret about this old lady." Her voice sounded weak and tired.

"Nana—"

"I need to rest my eyes for a few minutes." Her grandmother cut her off. "We can talk about it later dear, okay?"

"All right, Nana. I love you."

"I love you too."

Emmie swiped her phone screen, ending the call. She made a mental note to contact the hospital tomorrow during business hours, and get all the treatment details. Right now, she was just trying to process everything. *Cancer.* It was such an ugly word. A heaviness filled her heart and she closed her eyes. She, better than anyone, knew how quickly life could change.

God, please watch over my Nana. Let the tests be accurate and the doctors be smart.

A hard lump formed in the back of her throat, and she swallowed it down, pinching the bridge of her nose as she thought about what to do. The numbers from Mr. Harrison's offer flashed through her mind again. *It was a sign.*

She opened her phone app and dialed the number scrawled on the bottom of the card.

"Hello?" a gentleman's voice answered.

"Mr. Harrison, this is Emmie Walker. I've considered your offer and have decided to accept the position."

CHAPTER 3

Dorian sat in his office with his personal assistant Montgomery Harrison, and Kate Baker, the communications specialist, and pored over the tour manual that set forth the itinerary for his upcoming trip. He would be making multiple appearances throughout the United States and was pleased that none of them seemed over-the-top. They were very different in nature from the types of presentations Philip had made on his recent tour of Australia. As Dorian took in the different stops, a sense of excitement and pride filled him. This was just what he had needed. He glanced at his mother.

She met his gaze and gave him a small smile, and he knew she'd gone out of her way to choose venues he would enjoy. He returned her smile. *Maybe she did see him.*

"Security is already abroad," Kate said, flipping pages in the binder. The head of security, along with one of the bodyguards, was already in America checking each destination to coordinate every detail—from travel time to dress codes, as well as working with the appropriate officials to determine the best place for the royal motorcade to arrive at each location.

Dorian tried to pay attention as Kate went over a list of people the royal party would meet with and what etiquette needed to be discussed. She and Montgomery would be traveling with him, as well as a number of bodyguards. Venue plans were included in the tour manual to illustrate where everyone would stand, sit, and enter, and where the exits were located. He realized the information was important for safety reasons, but it was also mind-numbingly boring. If anything out of the ordinary happened, the likelihood of his remembering where the proper exit in a strange place was situated was next to zero. He knew his staff would take care of him and trusted them implicitly. As Kate droned on, Dorian's mind wandered to some of the locations he'd be visiting. His heart beat faster as his excitement over the possibilities grew.

"Howard will not be traveling with you to care for Gatsby," Montgomery said.

Dorian lifted his head, immediately alert. Howard had been the primary caretaker for Gatsby since Dorian received him as a small puppy. "What do you mean Howard can't go? He's always traveled with me."

"He's been talking about retiring and no longer wishes to travel."

"Retiring?" Dorian blinked. Howard had worked with the family's dogs since before Dorian was born.

Dorian couldn't imagine trusting Gatsby's care to anyone else.

Montgomery continued, "I have, however, taken the liberty of hiring a handler to travel with you."

Dorian took a deep breath and let it out slowly. Montgomery had been his personal assistant for as long as Dorian could remember, but sometimes the older man took liberties with his position that were not always warranted. This was one of those times.

Gatsby had been a gift from his late grandmother. Her corgis were her pride and joy and Gatsby was the top pick of her dog's last litter. Dorian adored the canine and thought of him as more of a child than a pet. He trusted Howard with Gatsby, and the thought of leaving the dog in the care of just *anyone* was daft. He pinned Montgomery with a piercing glare. "You hired someone to take care of Gatsby without conferring with me about it first?"

Kate shuffled papers and shifted uncomfortably in her seat.

"I would have preferred to be involved in the hiring process," Dorian said, his voice frigid.

Montgomery bowed his head in acknowledgment. "I understand. My apologies, Your Highness. However, I do assure you that she has impeccable references and came highly recommended."

"She!?"

Montgomery shot Kate a fleeting glance, then held Dorian's gaze. "Yes, *she*. As I said, she has impeccable references and has worked with corgis extensively. She arrived at the castle earlier today and is presently in the gardens working with Gatsby. I have her scheduled to meet with you later this evening."

Dorian bolted to his feet so fast his chair tipped over behind him. "She is here now? With Gatsby? Why wasn't I told?" He rushed out of the room without waiting to hear what Montgomery had to say and stormed through the halls of the castle toward the garden entrance. Though Dorian loved the furry little fellow, Gatsby wasn't always good with strangers. He wasn't about to have some strange woman upsetting his dog, not to mention the risk of losing him in the gardens. *He* didn't even take the dog into the gardens without a leash.

He shoved the iron gate leading into the garden open with such force that it slammed against the fence, ricocheted, and nearly hit him as he rushed through the opening. "Gatsby!" He called, rushing down the path toward the heart of the garden, his hands clenched into fists. Finding his dog was his top priority, then he'd deal with the trainer.

"Stay Gatsby," Emmie commanded and took a few steps backwards. The red and white Pembroke Welsh Corgi cocked his head and looked at her expectantly but didn't move. They were working outside in the royal garden. Emmie thought it would be easier to work with Gatsby one on one without the other dogs in the kennel distracting him, if you could call it a kennel. It was more like a state-of-the-art boarding facility than any kennel she'd seen.

The first part of her day was spent going over her contract with Montgomery and getting settled in what would be her room until they left on the tour in a couple of days. She planned to spend as much time with Gatsby as possible before their departure. The more time she had to work with him before they left, the easier it would be to handle him on the road. She wasn't sure how much training he'd had, but so far, he seemed like an intelligent, receptive dog.

Looking around at the impressive garden, Emmie fought off the urge to pinch herself to make sure she wasn't dreaming. Colorful, perfectly arranged flower beds lined the paved walkways that wound through the gardens. Tall trees with huge leafy canopies created pockets of shade, and she walked past a number of interesting sculptures as she and Gatsby made their way to the slightly more open area more suitable for training. The gardens were like nothing she'd ever seen. Sure, there were nice parks in the small town in Minnesota where she and her grandmother lived, but with the castle looming in the background, this was like something straight out of a fairy tale.

She stared at the imposing structure with its magnificent towers and spires. If someone had told her two weeks ago that she'd be staying in a 653 room castle, she'd have told them they were bonkers. Yet, here she was. Her room didn't face the garden, but she doubted she'd be able to pick which one of the many windows it was anyway. What would it be like to grow up in a castle? To have all that space?

The small trailer house she'd grown up in would fit many times over inside Dorburn Castle.

Emmie turned her attention back to the dog. He watched her with large, curious eyes. It was a good sign that he was eager to learn. She squatted down and held out a treat. "Come." He ran to her and sat, obediently waiting to receive his treat. "I think we're going to get along just fine, Gatsby." She stood and once again commanded the dog to stay while she backed away from him. Instead, the corgi's large ears shot up and he bounded off, disappearing down the pathway that led back to the castle.

"Gatsby! No!" Emmie sprinted after the dog. It was amazing how fast a dog with such short legs could run. She rounded a curve in the path and nearly collided with a man kneeling next to a very excited Gatsby. The man's back was to her, and she could hear him talking to the dog but wasn't able to make out what he was saying. She'd been assured by the man that ran the kennels that the garden would be a safe, quiet place to take Gatsby. She needed this job, if something happened to him...she shuddered at the thought. Whoever this was needed to leave.

"Do you mind? I'm trying to train this dog right now," she said, planting a hand on her hip.

The man that stood and turned to face her was easily the most attractive man Emmie had ever seen. He was very tall, but then compared to her own 5'2" frame, most people were. His long legs were clad in a pair of dark chinos, and he sported a tan short-sleeved button up shirt that hugged his broad shoulders. His wavy dark brown hair just touched the top of his collar, and his eyes were the most amazing shade of ocean blue. She found herself lost in them for just a second before recognition hit her like a bucket of ice water on a hot summer day. She'd just scolded Prince Dorian.

"Corn-nuts!" she blurted before she could stop herself, and immediately covered her mouth with her hands. She couldn't afford to let her lack of filter ruin this job for her.

The prince looked her up and down and several emotions played across his face, ranging from what looked like annoyance to amusement. She glanced down at the worn jeans, plain teal shirt, and sneakers she was wearing and her cheeks flooded with heat. If she had known there was any chance of running into the prince, she would have worn something more appropriate, although she wasn't really sure what that might be. Why couldn't her meeting with the communications specialist have been earlier? They were supposed to go over wardrobe requirements. Now, she stood in front of the most eligible bachelor in the world in training clothes. *Oh well, nothing she could do about it now. Might as well try to make the best of it.*

Gatsby was now jumping on her legs. Hoping she hadn't just lost this job, and not knowing quite what to say, she returned her attention to him, crouching to pat his head. "Gatsby, are you trying to get me in trouble? You need to listen to me, even when Dad is around," she gently scolded. The dog licked her hand and ran in excited circles between her and Prince Dorian.

Emmie stood and lifted her gaze. The prince was watching her with a half-smile that made her knees feel weak. No wonder the tabloids loved him. He was even better looking in person. She was dazed by his presence, but then something her grandmother used to say popped into her head. *Those celebrities put their pants on one leg at a time, Emmie, just like you do.* She exhaled slowly and tried to calm herself. He was just a man, like any other man. Who happened to be standing in front of *his castle. Ugh.*

"Corn-nuts?" he asked. His deep voice was gently amused.

"Yes, *corn-nuts.*" She gave him a tentative smile. "My grandmother taught me that swearing was for lazy people with a limited vocabulary and if I wanted to swear, I needn't be crude but creative."

Dorian returned her smile and took a step toward her, his large hand outstretched. "It certainly is creative. You must be Emmeline."

Even his accent was compelling; British tinged with something else she couldn't put her finger on. "Yes, I am. I'm pleased to meet you." She put her hand in his and the moment their palms touched, an odd, but pleasant sensation traveled through her. Her gaze met his again, lingering for a moment. She pulled her hand back. "And it's Emmie. Just Emmie."

"Okay, *Just Emmie*. You may call me Dorian."

Emmie smiled. "Not Your Highness or Your Grace? Are you sure? On TV, they always refer to royalty as 'Your Grace.' And I'm pretty sure Gatsby would be a duke. The Duke of Fluffington."

Dorian laughed, his deep baritone reverberating through the bushes. He looked even more incredible when he was laughing.

Emmie gave herself a mental kick in the rear to clear her thoughts. She needed to focus on the job. "I'm sorry for laying into you just now. I'm trying to do some groundwork with him before we leave on your trip." She pointed at Gatsby, who had assumed the typical corgi *sploot* pose at her feet. Flat on his belly with his back legs outstretched behind him and his front legs stretched out in front of him, Gatsby watched them intently.

Dorian looked from the corgi to her and nodded. "Yes, about that, we need to discuss some of the details."

Emmie put her hand up to stop him. Dorian wrinkled his brows. "Before we talk trip details, I need to know when I will have,"— she cleared her throat for emphasis and smiled—"*uninterrupted* time to work with Gatsby. It's important we have time to develop a trust relationship before we leave, or he won't respond well to me away from his comfort zone."

"He seems comfortable with you already." Dorian squatted down to pet Gatsby. "Aren't you, buddy?" Gatsby wagged his tail, then rested his head on his front paws and closed his eyes, clearly bored with their discussion. Dorian rose and stuck his hands in the pockets of his pants. "Which is really quite strange."

Emmie cocked her head to the side. "Why is that strange? I don't smell bad—or do I?"

"That's not what I meant at all. I think you smell lovely." His cheeks flamed red, and he shuffled his feet.

She raised a brow. *Was he flustered?*

"No, no, not lovely," he stammered. "What I mean is, I'm sure you smell fine. If I was close enough to smell you, that is." He shook his head. "Ugh, what was that you just said? Corn-nuts!"

They both laughed.

"What I'm trying very badly to say is that Gatsby doesn't usually take very well to strangers, women in particular. Yet"—Dorian glanced at the prone dog and back to Emmie again—"he seems quite enchanted with you."

"I don't know about enchanted, but we seem to have gotten off on the right foot...or paw."

They laughed again.

"Seriously Dorian—you're sure I can call you just Dorian?"

"Yes, *Just Emmie*."

Emmie rolled her eyes and tried not to laugh. *How was it possible this was the same person that Candace Easton had said was 'too stuffy for words'?*

"Okay, seriously, Dorian, I need time to work with him before we leave. I only have a couple of days and usually it takes much longer to develop a good training bond with a dog. Although, Gatsby appears to be very smart."

Hearing his name, Gatsby lifted his head to look up at Emmie and wagged his tail as if in agreement. He got up on all fours, stretched his feet out behind him one at a time and sat next to Emmie expectantly.

"See?" Emmie said. "He wants to learn."

Dorian slowly shook his head and ran his hands through his hair. "I've never seen him like this with anyone," he said in wonderment. His eyes softened. "You may have as much time with him as you require. I will see to it that you aren't disturbed."

"Does that include you?" Emmie clapped her hand to her mouth in horror. "I'm so sorry, I have this awful condition where words just fall out of my mouth before my brain has a chance to filter them."

Dorian chuckled. "It's actually quite refreshing to be around someone who isn't afraid to speak their mind in front of me."

Emmie hadn't thought about that. How awful it must be for him, not knowing if what was being said to him was genuine or just for show because of who he was. She didn't know what to say, so she simply nodded.

"And yes," he continued, "it does include me. I'll give you all the time you need. I trust Gatsby is in good hands with you. I will leave you to it then."

Dorian turned and began walking toward the castle then suddenly paused, turning back toward her. "My mother is hosting a small dinner party later this week in honor of the tour. I would like it if you attended. I'll have Montgomery give you the details."

He wanted her to have dinner with his mother. *His mother. The queen.* This had to be some really strange out-of-body experience she was having. "Sure, is the Pope coming too?"

Dorian grinned. "Not this time. I have a feeling this is going to be a much more interesting trip than I originally thought it would be." He headed toward the castle and as he walked away, he murmured, "I'm very much looking forward to it."

Emmie's gaze shifted to Gatsby, who stared at her with a playful expression. Emmie fanned herself with her hand and let out a long sigh. "So am I."

CHAPTER 4

Dorian couldn't understand the need for a 'Royal Send-off Dinner', but if anyone could create a reason for a party, it was his mother. Sophia loved her parties, and it was a well-known honor to be invited to one. She had assured him, however, that this would be a smaller, more intimate gathering with mostly family. She'd been shocked when he'd insisted Emmie attend, but had eventually acquiesced as this was a private, not public, gathering.

Dorian hadn't seen Emmie since he'd run into her in the gardens. True to his word, he made a special point of avoiding that area of the castle grounds. He also made sure she wasn't in the kennel area when he went to visit with Gatsby, although he had found himself checking in with security frequently to see where she was. For some reason, he seemed unable to get the feisty American trainer off his mind.

Dinner was held in the formal dining room, which contained a large cherrywood table that could comfortably accommodate nearly forty guests. Queen Sophia sat in her traditional place at the head of the table and wore a soft mint linen pantsuit rather than a gown. Her long dark hair was down for a change, flowing in soft waves around her shoulders and she wore no crown. Even without it, she looked regal. Dorian took his customary place next to Philip and groaned inwardly when he saw Ingrid seated directly across from him.

What is she doing here?

He shot his mother a questioning glance and, in response, she threw an innocent smile his way.

At least he would get a short break from her attempts at matchmaking while he was in America. Ingrid's mother, Lady Leticia, and Sophia had been best friends since they were children and Sophia considered Ingrid to be a perfect match for Dorian.

"Dorian, how lovely to see you again." Ingrid ran her fingers through her short, blonde hair like a parrot preening its plumage. She was dressed as though she'd intended to go to a club but ended up at a dinner party instead. He wouldn't doubt that was exactly what happened.

"Ingrid," he said stiffly. A sound by the door caught his attention. He turned toward the commotion and was pleasantly surprised to see Emmie rush into the room.

She wore black pants and a loose, dark blue shirt covered with a long floral duster. Her toffee brown hair had been up when he saw her in the garden, but now her sleek, smooth locks hung nearly to her waist. She had a slightly round face with large, honey-colored eyes fringed with long lashes and full, lush lips. A long, jagged scar ran from her chin along the left side of her face from the bottom of her chin up to the hairline just beside her eye. He'd noticed it earlier in the gardens. What could have caused such an injury? While obvious, the scar didn't detract at all from her natural beauty.

She made eye contact with him and her face flushed with embarrassment as the other guests turned to see who the tardy person was. Dorian realized her inexperience with royal protocol had put her at a disadvantage, and he regretted the awkward position he'd put her in. He stiffened. It shouldn't matter, this was supposed to be an informal dinner. He flashed her an encouraging smile.

Beside him, Philip quietly cleared his throat and gave Dorian a swift kick under the table. Dorian bristled, but bit his tongue. He supposed it *was* a bit untoward, inviting her to dinner with the family.

She was hired to attend to Gatsby, he reminded himself, but there was something about her that intrigued him.

"I'm so sorry I'm late." She pressed a hand to her throat, her cheeks still tinged a lovely shade of pink. "I got lost."

Ingrid sniffed with disapproval. His mother forced a polite, but perfunctory smile at Emmie. The queen abhorred tardiness for any reason.

"You must be Emmeline." Sophia gave Emmie an appraising look and waved a jewel-clad wrist in the air, summoning an attendant. "Please show her to her seat."

Dorian noticed that Emmie wisely had not corrected his mother with her preferred nickname and watched as she settled into the empty spot next to Ingrid. He was pleasantly surprised that Emmie hadn't dressed up for dinner with royalty. She was clearly comfortable being herself and he found that immensely appealing. Candace was an opportunist that had dressed and acted according to what she thought she might gain from the situation. Too bad he hadn't seen that right away. Ingrid was proving to be cut from the same cloth, and Dorian swore he would never allow someone like that to get close to him again.

Ingrid glanced disdainfully at Emmie as though she were a bug to be squashed and slowly, deliberately slid her place setting farther from Emmie's. Thankfully, Emmie didn't appear to notice. She was too busy staring up at the elaborate chandelier, her mouth gaping in awe. He glanced up and realized that as many times as he'd been in that room, he'd never really paid attention to how beautiful the fixture was. Come to think of it, he paid little attention to most of the lavishness around him. *That was something he would need to work on.*

"Wow, this is a really beautiful room, Your Majesty," Emmie said as she smiled at his mother.

"The whole castle is just amazing. I've never seen anything so wonderful."

"Yes," Queen Sophia agreed, appearing to relax somewhat. "We do take a great deal of pride in our home." She picked up her crystal wine goblet and held it up. "Thank you all for being here on the eve of this most auspicious trip to the United States. Dorian, we are all counting on you to represent Avington in the most positive light. Here's to your safe travel and your success. Bon voyage!"

"Bon voyage!" Everyone at the table responded, raising their glasses in a reciprocal toast. Immediately, the staff began serving the meal. The Queen picked up her fork and tasted her food. Once everyone followed her lead, she busied herself in conversation with Leticia.

Emmie smiled across the table at him. "Dorian, thank you for making yourself scarce while Gatsby and I have been working."

Ingrid choked on her wine. "Dorian?" she huffed.

Emmie looked at her, a confused expression on her face. "Well yes. That is his name, isn't it?"

Philip unsuccessfully tried to stifle a chuckle. Irritated, Dorian wished he could elbow his brother in the ribs.

"I'm glad to hear training has gone well," Dorian said to Emmie. "I trust you and Gatsby will be ready to leave in the morning?"

"She's going with you?" Ingrid cried. "That's ludicrous. I've never been to America. I'll go and watch Gumby for you."

Philip didn't even bother to try to hide his laughter this time. Dorian leaned back and shot him a warning glare. Over his dead body would Ingrid *ever* watch Gatsby. He opened his mouth to tell her just that, but Emmie cut him off.

"His name is Gatsby," Emmie enunciated slowly.

"Whatever," Ingrid said with a dismissive wave of her hand. "It's just a dog, it can't be *that* hard to watch a dog. Besides"— she gazed at Dorian, turning on a thousand-watt smile as she reached across the table to lay her hand on his— "it would give us plenty of alone time to spend together."

Dorian was speechless. What was with Ingrid and her little scheme of openly flirting in front of his mother? This was not good. He pulled away his hand and gripped the edge of the table. He needed a diversion and needed one fast.

Emmie's brow lifted at Ingrid's ridiculous suggestion. She leaned toward Ingrid and said with exaggerated sweetness, "I'm pretty sure if Dorian had wanted you to look after Gatsby, he wouldn't have hired me."

Dorian's jaw dropped. Ingrid forced a breath through clenched teeth and glared hard at Emmie. She opened her mouth to say who knows what, but was cut off by Philip.

"Dorian, were you at the polo match this afternoon?" Philip asked in a voice slightly louder than his usual tone.

Dorian blinked, momentarily confused before a wave of understanding came over him. He smiled gratefully at his brother. They didn't always get along, but Dorian knew deep down that Philip had his back when necessary. "Yes, it was a dandy."

The remainder of the meal went smoothly, and Emmie excused herself to pack immediately after the queen left the party. Dorian's gaze followed her out of the room.

"Be careful with that one, brother," Philip said under his breath so Ingrid wouldn't overhear. "She is an employee, which we both know means *off-limits.*"

Dorian absently nodded in agreement. He was right, of course. But Dorian never had been much of one for following the rules and this American trainer was going to make it very hard to stick to them.

"Gatsby, how is it possible you have a better wardrobe than I do?"

Emmie gazed down at the furry animal in wonder. She stood in the kennel in front of an armoire filled with every piece of clothing imaginable for a dog. She ran her fingers down what looked to be a tailored black tuxedo jacket. A small blue vest hung under it and a matching bow tie with an elastic neck band dangled from the hook of the hanger. There was a variety of shirts, hats, leashes, and a huge array of bow ties.

She made her selections and placed them carefully in Gatsby's monogrammed luggage. She was used to the excess that some of the dog show owners lavished on their precious pets, but this took it to an entirely different level. There was also a raised Baroque-style feeding bowl and stainless-steel fountain watering bowl that actually contained its own filter and purifier. Most of the food would be purchased in the United States, but there were vitamins and supplements to include as well.

Once she had Gatsby's wardrobe and essentials packed, Emmie busied herself going through the file drawer with his name, gathering the necessary paperwork and shot records he would need to get through customs and be allowed to enter certain venues.

Emmie had spent most of the morning with Kate going over the itinerary and what was expected of her. There were three basic rules: 1. Gatsby is the utmost priority; 2. Do not speak to the Prince unless required; 3. Stay away from the media.

She'd already had trouble with Rule 2 at dinner. She would have to try harder to keep herself in check. Focusing on the compensation she'd receive at the end of the job should help. She really needed the money. Her grandmother really needed the money. A ripple of guilt ran through her as she thought about her grandmother alone in the hospital, well, except for Agnes. Deciding she'd call her later, Emmie turned her attention back to the dog at her feet.

"You're going to end up with more luggage than I am," she told Gatsby, curling her legs under her on the plush rug that covered this area of the room. It was set up almost like a living room, with a short sofa and two lush overstuffed chairs. The corgi climbed into her lap and lavished her with sloppy kisses. Emmie laughed, "You are such a lucky dog to have an owner that loves you as much as your dad does."

"I would hope the feeling is mutual," a familiar baritone voice came from behind her.

Emmie spun around. Dorian leaned on the frame of the door, one long leg hooked casually over the other, his arms loosely crossed over his broad chest. How was it possible that he became better looking every time she saw him? *How was she supposed to follow the rules when he kept showing up?*

Gatsby leaped off her lap and ran to Dorian, jumping on his legs until Dorian bent to pick him up. The dog immediately settled in his arms and rested his head on Dorian's shoulder.

Emmie's heart skipped at least one beat. "Pretty sure you have nothing to worry about there. He's clearly crazy about you." She smiled. *Who could blame the dog?* She gave herself another mental kick. *Focus on the job, focus on the job.*

"I wanted to apologize for dinner," he said as he walked into the room and sat in one of the chairs. Gatsby sprawled upside down on his lap and Dorian absently rubbed his belly.

"Apologize for what?" Still sitting, Emmie folded her arms. "What did you do?"

Dorian lifted his shoulder in half a shrug, "Not me, for Ingrid. She can be. . ."

"A harpy?" Emmie slammed her eyes shut and shook her head. *Think before you speak!* "I'm sorry. That was uncalled for." She pulled her knees up to her chest and hugged them with her arms, resting her chin on top. "What's her deal though?"

Dorian pursed his lips and took a deep breath. "I've known Ingrid most of my life. She can be very persistent when she wants something."

"And she wants you."

Dorian nodded. "She thinks she does. She's not used to being told no."

"Hmm..." Emmie managed to stop herself before finishing her less than appropriate thought. She picked at a piece of dog hair on her pants. "Is she coming on the trip?"

Dorian snorted. His upper lip curled. "Not if I can help it." He shifted in the chair and leaned forward, placing Gatsby on the rug. The dog ran straight to Emmie and settled next to her. Dorian gave a wistful smile and stood. His gaze held hers for a long moment, an unreadable expression on his face. He cleared his throat and stepped toward the door. "I'll leave you to finish packing. Good night,

Just Emmie," he said with a quick smile. "I'll see you bright and early in the morning."

"Good night, Dorian." Emmie watched him leave as she slowly smiled to herself.

Yes, you will.

CHAPTER 5

The flight from Avington to the Ronald Reagan Washington National Airport, although long, had been uneventful for the most part. Emmie was surprised when she learned they'd be flying commercial. She'd assumed the Prince would travel by private jet, but he'd told her the Council preferred the family to fly commercial whenever possible.

Kate had explained that the Council acted much like a governing body. While the Queen was the monarch of Avington, the Council served as an advisory board and was in charge of several regulatory functions. Most of it was over Emmie's head, but she'd found it interesting how their government differed from what she was used to in the States.

The group occupied most of the airline's first-class section, and even Gatsby had his own seat. The only disruption during the flight was when they'd hit some turbulence and Trevor, one of Dorian's bodyguards, had gotten sick.

Emmie had been seated between Gatsby and Kate and despite several attempts at conversation with the older woman, Emmie eventually gave up and read or slept through the remainder of the flight. She had fully stocked her e-reader with cozy mysteries the night before and enjoyed the quiet reading time, so she wasn't bothered by Kate's lack of interest in chatting. *Was she even capable of small talk?* Emmie didn't think so.

Dorian sat farther up, next to Montgomery, and it sounded like they were discussing the itinerary in great detail. He'd glanced back, as if to check on her several times, but remained at the front of the plane. It was just as well; she needed to work harder at not consorting with him.

Once they landed and deplaned, Emmie gripped Gatsby's leash and led him to the waiting limo. She climbed in and situated Gatsby in his special car seat. The dog truly had everything. She settled back into the leather seat next to him and peered out the window.

Dorian was still talking with the throng of reporters in front of the airport. One nice thing about traveling with royalty was not having to wait at the baggage claim area for their luggage. Emmie hated that; the crowds of people standing around always made her somewhat uncomfortable. Montgomery and Trevor were taking care of it. Kate and the other two bodyguards, Brody and Chet, were with Dorian. She'd traveled quite a bit while working with Bernie, but never with an entourage, and it would take some getting used to, especially the bodyguards. She'd known, of course, that Dorian would have them, but they were rarely in view at the castle.

Dorian waved goodbye to the reporters and crawled into the limo, taking the seat next to Emmie. The rest of their group climbed in after him. Once everyone was seated, they sped off toward their hotel. Emmie was looking forward to getting settled in her room and hoped she'd have the luxury of taking a hot bath.

"Did you enjoy your nap?" Dorian asked.

Emmie creased her brows. *Nap?*

"I went back to check on you during the flight and you were napping. I didn't want to wake you, so I returned to my seat."

"It was fine. Thank you," she replied, pulling her hair over her shoulder and fiddling with Gatsby's collar. *Don't consort.*

"Between you, Gatsby and Kate, I'm not sure which of you were snoring louder." Dorian crinkled his nose in the most adorable way.

Gatsby and Kate shot him a dirty look, but Emmie couldn't help a little giggle. "Oh honey, don't you know? Women don't snore, we purr."

Dorian's mouth opened and abruptly closed, as though he was tempted to say something, but decided to keep it to himself. Montgomery and the three bodyguards tried to stifle their laughter as Kate's mouth gaped in abject horror.

"That's entirely inappropriate," Kate chided, her red lipstick-lined mouth clamped in a thin line. Emmie suddenly realized who Kate reminded her of—Meryl Streep's portrayal of Miranda in the movie *The Devil Wears Prada*, only Kate was not nearly as fashion forward.

"You're absolutely right, Ms. Baker," Emmie agreed. She turned to Dorian with a wide grin.

"Your Highness, it's quite inappropriate to tell a lady she snores in public."

Kate harrumphed and turned away, muttering something to Montgomery about rude Americans.

Dorian sat with his large hands covering his face, his head shaking.

Emmie's mouth twisted, along with her gut. *Maybe she'd taken it a little too far.*

Dorian brought his hands down, his lips clamped together in an obvious attempt to look stern. It wasn't working. "You are incorrigible," he admonished with a smile.

"No," Emmie frowned. "It's like I said before, I think my filter is broken. I know I'm supposed to keep my mouth shut," she lamented. "But it's like somebody else takes over my mouth and the words just tumble out."

"What do you mean, you're supposed to keep your mouth shut?"

She stole a quick glance at Kate, who was deep in conversation with Montgomery. She didn't look happy. Did she ever look happy? Emmie turned back to Dorian and quoted from memory, using a soft voice. "Rule number two, do not speak to the prince unless required." It had been her mantra the last two days.

Dorian's brows knit together. "Who told you that?"

Emmie lifted her chin, jerking it in Kate's direction, but said nothing.

Dorian glanced over at the older woman and shook his head. He leaned toward Emmie and lowered his voice, "You're taking care of the most important member of this trip. You can talk to me anytime. About anything. You understand?"

Emmie stared into his deep blue eyes and at first, couldn't seem to pull away. She nodded slowly, barely aware she was responding.

"Good." Dorian settled back into his seat. They rode the rest of the way to the hotel in comfortable silence.

The hotel was actually a series of luxury townhouses situated around a large, fountained garden. After letting Gatsby take care of his business, Emmie made her way into the townhouse and was taken aback by the luxury. The door opened into a large foyer with an open staircase leading upstairs, and a huge chandelier hung from the high ceiling. She toed off her shoes and her feet sank into the plush beige carpet. It was very different from the worn shag carpet she'd grown up with. She unclipped Gatsby's leash and followed the dog into the living area.

A full kitchen with stainless steel appliances and granite countertops filled half of the room, along with an adjoining formal dining area. The other half contained a living room with overstuffed leather furniture, a huge flat-screen television, a sliding glass door that led to a patio, and an inset gas fireplace. There were two closed doors off the living room, and Emmie assumed they were bedrooms. When Kate had told her that they would all be staying in the same suite, she initially balked at the idea, but Kate assured her they would each have a separate room. She wasn't kidding.

"I've taken the liberty of having Gatsby's luggage placed in your room, Miss Walker, which you will find upstairs," Montgomery said, indicating toward the stairs with his hand. He gave her a kind smile. "I think you'll find it to your liking. Dorian and the boys will be staying on this level. The rest of us, including myself, will be staying upstairs." Emmie nodded her thanks, smirking at the way Montgomery referred to the bodyguards as "the boys". With their hulking physiques, they were anything but.

Because of the time difference, it was still early afternoon in Washington, DC. Dorian had disappeared into his room of the townhouse to change. He had a meeting scheduled for later in the afternoon with members of Congress at Capitol Hill. Emmie knew from going over the itinerary that she would not be required to take Gatsby to this meeting, as dogs were not allowed at Congress.

She decided to go up the stairs to her room and retrieve Gatsby's necessities. Her room had a king size bed and a private bathroom with a Jacuzzi tub. *I'll definitely make use of that later*, she vowed and let out a sigh as she visualized herself sinking into a warm stream of swirling bubbles. After the long flight, that would feel so amazing.

Gathering Gatsby's food and water containers, dry food and supplements, she went back downstairs to feed him. Before they'd departed, she had given Montgomery a list of names of the local pet supply stores in each town they were planning to stay, and he'd sent one of the bodyguards out to pick up the fresh food he normally ate. Until he returned, she'd give the dog a little bit of dry kibble to hold him over.

Dorian emerged from his bedroom in a dark grey suit. His dark curls were still slightly damp from the shower, and he was knotting a crimson tie around his neck. He looked up and flashed her a grin.

"Are you settling in all right?"

"Yes, I'm just getting ready to give Gatsby some food. I'm sure he's hungry after having to fast before his airplane ride." Upon hearing his name and seeing her work with his food bowls, the dog spun in excited circles. "Hang tight, Duke," Emmie laughed. "I'm getting your food ready."

"Duke?" Dorian raised his eyebrows as he fastened his cufflinks.

"Yes," Emmie said. She placed Gatsby's feeding mat on the floor, and carefully set his bowls on the mat. Gatsby ran to the bowls, sniffed, and lifted his head. He looked at Emmie in disgust. She glanced at Dorian and shrugged her shoulders. "The Duke of Fluffington, who is apparently too good for his kibble."

Dorian chuckled. "He definitely has high-end taste. I trust Montgomery has gone out to get his food?"

"I believe he sent Trevor, who should be back shortly. I just thought I would give Gatsby a little something since it's been a while since he's eaten."

"Is the room to your liking?"

"The room is lovely, thank you. This whole place is just. . .grand. I think you could fit our apartment back home in here three times over."

"I'm glad it pleases you." Dorian paused for a moment, his forehead creasing. "Our?" he finally asked.

"Yes, I share, well shared, a small apartment with my grandmother. She hasn't been feeling well for the last several months, so she's in an assisted living facility now." Emmie stopped herself before giving out more information. He didn't need to know about her grandmother's failing health.

"Ah," he said. He paused, then drew his brows together. "I'm sorry to hear that. Hope it's nothing serious."

"Me too," Emmie said softly. She'd spoken to her grandmother's care team daily, and they'd confirmed the diagnosis of lung cancer. It was an aggressive type of cancer and had already metastasized. While they could try chemotherapy and radiation, it wouldn't buy much time and true to form, Nana had refused anyways. "The good Lord will take me when it's my time with or without pumping my body full of chemicals," she'd said when Emmie tried to argue with her about it.

The circumstances made being away even harder, but it was just a few weeks and she'd be able to dote on Nana when she returned home. Blanche's friend, Agnes, had promised to visit daily and that helped ease Emmie's mind too. While Agnes might be a little eccentric, she was a good friend.

Montgomery entered the kitchen checking his watch. "Your Highness, the car is ready. Chet and Brody are waiting."

"I'll be right out," Dorian said. He ran his hand through his hair and straightened the lapel on his jacket. On his way out, he paused. "Kate will make sure you have everything you need, Emmie."

Emmie rolled her eyes and gave him a cheesy smile. "I'm sure she will."

Dorian laughed. "If you go anywhere, make sure you take Trevor with you." He bent down and gave Gatsby a quick pat on the head. "And you be good for her. I'll bring you a special treat when I come back, buddy."

"Have fun!" Emmie called as Montgomery and Dorian walked out the door. Dorian glanced back and gave her a small wave before closing the door behind him.

Emmie finished feeding Gatsby and returned to her room to relax for a while. She had planned to take the dog for a walk but wanted to give her Nana a call first. She pulled her cell phone out of her purse and dialed the number. The phone rang several times, but there was no answer. Emmie quickly looked up the phone number for the hospital on her browser app and pressed the call button. A couple of transfers later, the phone was now ringing in her grandmother's room.

"Hello?" Nana's voice sounded weak on the other end of the line. Emmie's heart sank.

"Nana? It's Emmie. How are you doing?"

"Emmie! They're holding me prisoner here."

"Agnes assured me you were going to get out yesterday. I thought she would've called if plans had changed. Are you okay?" Emmie made a mental note to contact Agnes after she was done talking to her grandmother. She needed to be aware of what was going on while she was away.

"Oh, don't be mad at Agnes. I told her not to call you. I knew you would be busy with your prince. I want you to tell me all about that."

"He's not my prince, Nana," Emmie said. "I'm watching his dog, remember?"

"Same thing. He's there, isn't he?"

"I suppose that's true. It's fine, we're in Washington, DC. He's meeting with some members of Congress right now and I'm just hanging out in the room at the townhouse we've rented. You wouldn't believe it, Nana. This place is bigger than our whole apartment. It's got a nice garden in the front with a fountain. I know how much you like fountains."

"I'm glad you're enjoying yourself. I want to hear about this prince, though. It's not every day my only granddaughter is hobnobbing with royalty. What's he like?"

"I don't know him very well yet, but so far he's been very nice to me."

"Nice, schmice," Nana said. "I don't want to hear that he's nice. I want to hear if he's hot."

"Nana!" Emmie laughed. Her grandmother might be seventy-two years old, but she was more up to date with current culture than Emmie was most of the time.

"Well, is he?"

"He's easy on the eyes," Emmie admitted. "But that's not why I'm here. Besides, it doesn't matter if he's hot or not, he's a prince. I'm a dog handler."

"Is he single?" her grandmother asked.

"Yes. What difference does that make?"

"If he's single, it matters."

"I don't know about that. He is nice to talk to, although I've probably said more than I should have a few times. You know what a hard time I have not saying what's on my mind," Emmie laughed ruefully.

"You just be you, Emmie. Never put on airs for anyone."

Nana erupted in a fit of coughing on the other end of the phone.

"Are you okay, Nana?"

"They're running more tests," she said, her voice sounding weak. "I'm just tired. Really tired."

"I'll let you go then. Get some rest. I'll call you again soon. I love you, Nana."

"You don't worry about those words that come out of your mouth. You just make sure they're genuine. I love you too, sweet girl."

Emmie slid her finger across the screen, disconnecting the call as her eyes filled with tears. It broke her heart that she couldn't be at the hospital with her grandmother, especially now. She was more determined than ever to do the best job she could so she could hurry back to Minnesota to help her get better.

CHAPTER 6

Dorian adjusted the light grey beret on his head and picked his white gloves off the dresser in his room at the hotel. Those would go on at the last possible moment. He inspected his ceremonial uniform in the mirror one last time before he left for Arlington National Cemetery. The forest green sash was in place over his shoulder and his pins were all straight. His jacket and pants were a very dark blue, almost black, and any stray hairs from Gatsby showed off like they were under a black light. Not seeing anything out of place, he stepped into the living room of the townhouse.

Kate sat in the formal dining area on the phone, no doubt confirming the press schedule for the day. Chet, Trevor, and Brody were seated at the long counter in the kitchen eating, while Montgomery watched the news in the living room. Where were Emmie and Gatsby? He was just about to ask when a sharp, excited bark came from upstairs. Knowing he shouldn't go near the dog before he left, but unable to help himself, Dorian climbed the stairs. He hadn't been up here since their arrival the day before. By the time he'd returned the night before after his meetings on Capitol Hill and the Senator's dinner he'd been obligated to attend, the townhouse had been quiet.

He followed the happy dog noises down the hallway until he reached a partially opened door. He glanced inside. Emmie sat cross-legged on the floor of her room with a brightly colored plastic toy tray on the carpet in front of her. Gatsby's tail wagged like it was a propeller, and he pushed at the toy with his snout. Dorian leaned in to get a closer look, his eyes widening as Gatsby slid a compartment of the tray open with his nose, revealing a treat. The dog gave an excited yip, gobbled up the morsel, then gazed at Emmie expectantly.

"Good job Gatsby! Give me five!" Emmie cheered, holding out her palm. The corgi slapped his furry paw on it.

When did he learn how to do that? Gatsby noticed him just then and scampered toward him. Dorian held out his arms to block the dog from getting too close to his dark uniform trousers.

"Gatsby, stop. Sit," Emmie commanded. The dog stopped in his tracks and obeyed. Dorian's jaw went slack. Gatsby was a smart dog but had never been good at following directions. This was amazing.

"What kind of magic have you worked on my dog?"

Emmie's head snapped up and wrinkles of surprise appeared on her forehead. Her gaze swiftly traveled from his polished shoes to his beret, then settled on his face. At a loss for words, her mouth opened, closed and opened again. A pink tinge colored her cheeks. "Um...ah..." she stammered. "M-magic?"

Dorian wasn't sure what to make of her reaction. She'd never acted that way with him before. Was she intimidated by his uniform?

"Yes. It must be magic. He has never been so obedient." He grinned and bent to carefully pet the dog's head before he stood, checking the bottom of his sleeve for any stray hairs.

"Right, magic," she said absently. She blinked several times, then shook her head and said, "Wait—not magic. We've been working really hard. Did you see him playing with the puzzle?" Her eyes sparkled with excitement.

"Is that what that is? I thought it was some kind of toy. I've never seen anything like it."

"It's a puzzle to stimulate the dog's mind. You put treats in the little compartments, and the dog has to use his nose and his brain to figure out how to open them in order to get the reward." She placed a little morsel in one of the compartments and closed the lid, then told Gatsby to find it. The dog sniffed the puzzle, immediately zoned in on the compartment where she had hidden the treat and shoved at it with his nose. The compartment flipped open, and Gatsby snatched the food.

Dorian laughed. "That's amazing. He's a genius."

Emmie laughed. "He thinks so, too." She glanced down at herself then back to him, and scrunched her nose. "I wasn't expecting to see you this morning. I'm still in my training clothes. Good thing you didn't bring reporters."

Dorian chuckled. She wore black yoga pants covered in dog hair and a simple T-shirt. Her long hair was pulled into a ponytail, and she didn't appear to be wearing any makeup. None of the women he knew would be caught dead like that, let alone in his presence. He thought she looked better in her training clothes than most of them looked in their dress clothes. With her short sleeves, he noticed another long, ropelike scar on her left arm. He was curious, but was hesitant to ask her about it. Deciding to leave it for another time, he gave her a playful grin.

"I'm disappointed. I surely thought you trained Gatsby in a ball gown."

"You couldn't afford to pay me to work in a ball gown," Emmie said with a laugh, then furrowed her brows. "That's a pretty impressive uniform. I didn't realize you were in the military."

Dorian was pleasantly surprised. He wasn't used to being around people who didn't know every single detail about him. It was refreshing. It made him feel like a regular person to her, not *Prince Dorian*.

"Yes, my brother Philip and I both served in the military."

Emmie called Gatsby to come sit in her lap and she stroked the dog's fur. "What did you do in the military? I mean...What was your job?"

Dorian leaned into the doorframe and crossed his arms. "Well, my official title is Captain, but I was a gunner."

Emmie gasped. "A gunner? What is that...exactly?"

"I co-piloted a helicopter, an Apache to be specific. I was a weapons operator."

Emmie's mouth formed a small O, then she went silent for a moment. "Did you have to fly in any wars?" she asked softly.

Dorian shifted away from the doorframe letting his arms fall to his sides. He didn't care to talk about the tour he did in Afghanistan. It was part of his duty, but not something he chose to carry with him. "Yes," he said simply.

"I'm so sorry you had to go through that." Emmie brushed a stray hair behind her ear and a pensive expression crossed her face. "One of my best friends from high school died in Afghanistan." Sadness filled her eyes and she shifted her gaze from his, turning her attention to the dog on her lap. She leaned down to place a quick kiss on Gatsby's head. "Your dad is sure brave," she murmured to the dozing animal.

The flash of pain he saw in her eyes when she mentioned her friend hit him like a blow to his heart. "I'm really sorry about your friend," he said. He knew that feeling all too well as he'd lost someone close to him there too.

Emmie nodded, her honey eyes curiously fixed on his. He was unable to pull his gaze away. Dorian didn't think he'd ever seen anyone so beautiful in his life, and that scared him more than any tour he had ever done in the military.

"Your Highness," Montgomery called from the bottom of the stairs, bringing Dorian out of his trance. "The car is ready. It's time to leave for Arlington."

Emmie and Gatsby weren't accompanying him to the cemetery. Gatsby was deathly afraid of the cannons and Dorian knew that was part of the ceremony. "That's my cue."

Emmie smiled. "Good luck at Arlington, I've heard it's amazing."

"Thank you, Emmie. I'm sorry that you and Gatsby can't come with me." To his surprise, Dorian found he actually meant that.

DORIAN ARRIVED AT ARLINGTON National Cemetery. Several high-ranking officials from each branch of the U.S. Military greeted him and escorted him through the cemetery. Members of several different media outlets hung back, but their presence was hard to miss. Dorian had never been to Arlington and the photos didn't do justice to the massive cemetery.

Dorian learned that Arlington contained over six hundred acres of meticulously maintained grounds. He observed full, tall trees lining the narrow roads that led in a maze throughout the vast property. Varieties of trees he'd never seen before. Countless rows of simple, white marble headstones lined up like soldiers on parade, covered the manicured lawn. Words could not describe the magnificence of this place.

They walked to Section 60, where veterans of the wars in Iraq and Afghanistan were laid to rest. Dorian placed a large, colorful wreath of flowers there to honor his comrades in arms. He'd handwritten a note and placed it in the center of the wreath, then posed for the requisite photo ops.

Afterwards, Dorian spent some time alone, walking through the rows and rows of white headstones.

His mood quickly sobered as he recalled his tour in Afghanistan and the friends and squad members he'd lost there, as well as Emmie's friend. He stopped in front of a marker of a young man, just two years younger than himself. Killed in action. His head tipped back for a moment and he closed his eyes. There was so much to be thankful for. He vowed to focus on that, rather than what he thought he might be missing.

The group continued through the cemetery. A large crowd of people gathered near the Tomb of the Unknown Soldier to watch the wreath placing ceremony. The mood was somber and the crowd quiet. So much of Dorian's life was pomp and circumstance and he usually felt like he was just going through the motions, but this was different. He was proud to be here. Proud to be representing Avington, and his family.

A full four platoon Honor Guard marched with him to the tomb. Avington's flag furled in the light breeze next to the stars and stripes of the American flag behind him. The Major General of the U.S. Army escorted him to the tomb. Dorian placed a large wreath of poppies on the tomb to honor the American soldiers lost in foreign wars; the service, sacrifice, and valor of their lives and the lives of those still serving. It was incredibly humbling. A lump formed in his throat as a solitary bugler played the lingering notes of Taps.

As Dorian stood there, a plan formed in his mind. With his status and resources, he could do many good things for the soldiers that did make it back home alive, as well as for the families of the ones that didn't. He could make a difference. Dorian found himself wishing Emmie was there to share this with him, then quickly pushed that thought aside. She was there to care for Gatsby, and only while he was in the United States. Not only was she an American, she was a citizen. Anything more than friendship with her could never work.

CHAPTER 7

"What do you mean Dorian wants Gatsby to come to the Veterans Hospital?" Emmie sat up, her eyes sparkling. She'd been lounging on the couch in the living room watching a rerun of Julia Love's cooking show on FoodTV with Gatsby. It was one of her favorite shows and she wasn't scheduled to bring the corgi anywhere today.

"I don't know what's going on," Kate said with a huff. "All I know is His Highness called and said he wanted Gatsby brought to the hospital. If he wants Gatsby, Gatsby goes, and if Gatsby goes, you go. We leave in fifteen minutes."

Emmie's heart sang. She planned to take Gatsby to the dog park a little later and maybe do some window shopping. Dorian was scheduled to be gone the entire day, and while she knew it would make more work for the rest of his staff, this change in schedule meant she'd get to spend extra time with him. She bent down to ruffle Gatsby's ears. "Did you hear that, Duke? You get to go see Dad." Gatsby began jumping around excitedly, as if he knew what Emmie had said.

"Could you please settle him down? I don't care to get dog hair all over my skirt," Kate snapped, stepping away from the dog.

"You don't like dogs much do you, Kate?"

Kate regarded her for a moment, then pinched her lips into a thin line, "No. I do not. I prefer cats. However, it is my job to tolerate all the royal family's dogs." She strode toward the stairs, pausing at the bottom step. "You may call me Ms. Baker." With that, she turned on her heel and disappeared up the stairs.

Emmie made eye contact with Montgomery, who'd been sitting in the dining room going through some paperwork. She grimaced and shrugged, which made the older man smile. Kate, make that *Ms. Baker*, had thwarted every attempt Emmie had made at conversation thus far. Turning her attention back to the excited dog at her feet, she stood. "Come on buddy, we need to get ready." The dog followed her up the stairs and into her room.

Emmie stared at the clothes she'd hung in the closet, trying to decide what was appropriate to wear to the Veterans Hospital. Kate had specifically informed her that she needed to dress up for any public events. Was this considered a public event? Emmie preferred to wear pants because they covered the thick scars on her leg. She finally decided on a pair of light tan slacks and a loose-fitting, pale turquoise chiffon blouse. After she'd changed her clothes, she slipped on her new brown wedge boots. She'd found them at a designer shoe warehouse while shopping for new clothes to wear on this trip. It was the first time Emmie had found tall boots that would accommodate her wide calves and she loved them.

She ran a brush through her long hair and applied just a touch of mascara and lip gloss. She had never been much of one for makeup, even when she was younger. Now, at twenty-five, Emmie couldn't see taking the time to learn how to use more than just the minimal amount she already used. Taking one last look in the mirror, she was satisfied with what she saw.

She reached back into the closet and grabbed Gatsby's forest green tote that bore his monogram and filled it with his camouflage bow tie, an extra leash, his traveling water bowl, a bottle of water, and a box of treats. Was this what it was like to pack for a child?

The ride to the Veterans Hospital was uneventful. Gatsby snored in his special car seat and Emmie was content to gaze out the window. She'd never been in D.C. before and was trying to make as many mental memories as she could so she could share them with Nana when she got home. Kate and Montgomery were going over last-minute plans and Trevor sat stoic and silent, as usual. She'd tried engaging all of the bodyguards in conversation but quickly learned they were even less talkative than Kate.

The limo arrived in front of a massive steel and glass structure. Emmie knew the famous hospital was big but wasn't prepared for just how enormous of a place it was. She unclipped Gatsby from his car seat and slid on his camouflage bow tie. He sat still while she adjusted it and snapped on his leash. One thing she'd learned about corgis on the dog show circuit was they could rock a bow tie; Gatsby was no exception. She waited for Trevor's signal to leave the vehicle, having learned that one must never get out of the vehicle before being told, and one must never close the car door after getting out. *So many rules.*

Emmie and Gatsby stepped out of the limo, and she immediately recognized Brody waiting by the door leading into the hospital. Dorian had one bodyguard with him at all times, and the second was on hand to wait at the doors or act as crowd control, depending upon the situation. When Emmie had asked Montgomery why Dorian had three bodyguards on the trip when he only brought two with him to his appearances, she was informed that Trevor was Gatsby's bodyguard. She'd started to laugh, but then realized Montgomery was serious. She was still flabbergasted that a dog would have its own bodyguard. How did Dorian and his family ever get used to having them around all the time? Every time she turned around, one of them was there. It was unnerving.

Emmie followed Montgomery and Kate through the doors of the hospital and into the huge atrium.

A gleaming black grand player piano softly played classical music next to a series of modern art water fountains. An elaborately decorated glass dome made up the ceiling, which allowed natural light to fill the area. It was simply beautiful.

Gatsby tugged on his leash and Emmie turned to see what had caught the dog's attention. Her heart lurched as she saw Dorian walking toward them, the corners of his mouth curled upward in a wide grin. He had changed out of his ceremonial uniform and was now dressed in his desert camouflage military fatigues and combat boots. The man was ridiculously attractive no matter what he was wearing. *You're here for Gatsby, not the prince*, she reminded herself for the five-hundredth time.

"Hi, thanks for accommodating the last-minute change in schedule," Dorian said, stopping in front of Emmie and stooping to rub the fur on Gatsby's head.

"It's fine. We were in the middle of binge-watching a cooking show. I mean, I'll never know how to make tiramisu now, but when the prince calls..." Emmie smiled and rolled her eyes in mock annoyance.

Dorian chuckled, then tilted his head to one side, an eyebrow raised. "We?"

"Yes, *we*. Gatsby learned how to make a frittata. I think he's going to try to take over the head chef's job once you return to Avington."

"Is that so?" Dorian directed his question to the corgi, who stared up at him with big, brown adoring eyes. Emmie could swear she saw a look of relief pass over his face.

A short grey-haired gentleman dressed in a dark military dress suit laden with medals and badges approached them. "I see the rest of your party has arrived, Your Highness."

"Yes," Dorian said, indicating toward Kate, "my communications secretary, Kate Baker."

Kate clutched her binder to her chest and gave a curt nod. Dorian moved his hand toward Montgomery. "Montgomery Harrison, my assistant." Montgomery shook the man's outstretched hand. Dorian then turned his hand toward Emmie. "And this is Emmeline Walker, Gatsby's handler."

Emmie stuck her hand out and gave the man a firm handshake. "Pleased to meet you, sir."

Dorian's gaze cut to hers. He gave Emmie a little whisper of a smile and continued, "This is Major Andrew Greene. He's going to be showing us around today."

"This must be Gatsby?" The major bent and nervously held his hand in front of Gatsby's nose.

Emmie noticed Dorian's posture tense. She remembered him telling her that Gatsby could be slightly unpredictable around strangers. She made quick eye contact with Dorian and raised her hand, lifting her forefinger to indicate she had this. She then crouched next to Gatsby. She'd been working with the dog on a new trick and hoped he'd remember it. "Gatsby, can you greet Major Greene? Greet," Emmie softly commanded.

Gatsby sat up on his haunches and offered a paw for the man to shake. The major accepted his paw and gently lifted it in a quick shake. Standing, the major looked at Emmie, "That's a well-trained dog, Miss Walker. You do fine work."

Emmie beamed at the compliment and turned toward Dorian. He was standing with his jaw hanging and she wasn't quite sure what to make of the expression on his face.

The major began walking and Dorian took a place next to him, with Emmie and Gatsby bringing up the rear. Brody and Chet flanked them, and Emmie noticed Trevor was now posted at the door of the main entrance. Kate had returned to the main office with Montgomery to facilitate the photo shoot after the hospital tour. Emmie returned her attention to the front and Dorian glanced back at her, giving her a quick smile and a thumbs-up before they entered the rehabilitation wing of the hospital. Emmie suppressed a giggle. *Princes didn't give thumbs-ups, did they?*

The rehabilitation center was beyond Emmie's imagination. There was every type of exercise equipment imaginable, including many pieces she didn't recognize. The room was enormous. Physical therapists, wearing light blue scrubs, were assisting a number of men and women with various activities. Major Greene explained the history of the rehab center to Dorian as Emmie stood off to the side, staying out of the way as much as she could.

Dorian turned to her and reached for Gatsby's leash, "Let's meet some soldiers, buddy."

Emmie placed the leash in his outstretched hand and his fingers momentarily curled around hers. A tingle coursed through her, and she pulled her hand away as the heat of a blush spread across her cheeks.

Dorian's gaze held hers for a moment before he broke away and followed the major with Gatsby. Unsure of what to do, she decided to stand where she was and wait. "Do not engage with the public." Kate's words echoed in her head as Dorian glanced back over his shoulder and motioned for her to follow. She trotted to catch up with them. If Dorian wanted her to follow him, she would.

Emmie watched with unabashed fascination as Dorian interacted with the wounded and recovering soldiers. He took time to speak with each one of them and seemed genuinely interested in hearing their stories. He spoke words of encouragement and thanked each of them for their service. He even shared stories with one soldier whose unit served alongside the same Avington unit he served in. Several soldiers had family members with them, who had obviously been invited for the occasion of meeting the prince. The few children there were enamored with Gatsby, and the dog relished the extra attention. Dorian visited with the families, gave hugs and posed for snapshots. Seeing the gratitude in their eyes as he took the time to talk to them individually warmed Emmie's heart toward him even more. The more time she spent with Dorian, the more she realized the tabloids painted a very inaccurate portrait of the man.

A short while later, after all the photos had been taken and goodbyes said, Emmie slid into the limo once again to head back to the townhouse. She clipped Gatsby into his car seat and slipped him a treat. "Way to go, Gatsby." She held out her hand and the dog lifted his paw to it in a high-five gesture. She ruffled the fur around his ears and settled back into the seat.

The door opened and Dorian slid in next to her. Brody followed. Once they were settled, the limo took off. Emmie gave Dorian a quizzical glance. He wasn't supposed to be riding in this car.

"Kate and Montgomery took the other car since we already had both of them here. I don't think Kate's very happy with me for deviating from the schedule," Dorian said with a smirk, "but she'll get over it."

Emmie chuckled. "You're pretty brave."

"I don't know about that." Dorian leaned toward her, resting his elbows on his knees. "I do know that I can't believe what you've done with Gatsby in such a short time."

As Emmie met Dorian's gaze, she rubbed her neck with her hand and swore she could feel her heart pounding under her palm. She cleared her throat and tried to refocus on why she was there. "That's what you hired me to do," she said. "He's a really smart dog. He just needed a little bit of fine-tuning."

Dorian settled back into the leather seats, resting the foot of his left leg on the knee of his right. He clasped his hands in his lap and let out a long sigh. "I'm beginning to think we could all use some fine-tuning."

CHAPTER 8

Dorian stood looking through the large windows into the courtyard and watched Emmie walking with Gatsby. Trevor walked by her side, and the two were having an animated conversation. A burning sensation filled Dorian's stomach at the sight of Emmie laughing with the man, and he tried to swallow it down. He rubbed the back of his neck and turned to Montgomery, who had just asked him about the deviation at the Veterans Hospital.

"I thought having Gatsby there would help bridge the gap with the soldiers." Since when did he have to give justification for changing plans, especially when it came to plans with Gatsby? He took a deep breath and let it out slowly. "In fact, I've decided to have him accompany me to the Children's Hospital in Memphis as well."

Montgomery pursed his lips, then asked, "Are you certain, Your Highness? With all the children, it could be a liability with Gatsby. Not to mention we have to make sure there are no allergies."

Dorian narrowed his eyes. "You saw Gatsby at the military hospital. Emmie has done wonders with him. I have no doubt that he will be fine with the children," he said. Dorian's pulse quickened and he fought not to grind his teeth. "Therapy dogs are in and out of hospitals all the time and don't need special clearance." Gatsby had accompanied him on every trip he'd ever taken, without question. What was the issue on this trip? He studied Montgomery for a moment. Dorian had known him nearly his entire life and could tell when the older man was holding something back.

"What's the real issue, Montgomery?" Dorian asked matter-of-factly.

Montgomery lowered his head for a moment and then met Dorian's gaze. "Miss Walker was in some of the press pictures from the military hospital."

Dorian closed his eyes and let his head fall back. Some days he wished he was just a normal man without the responsibilities and difficulties that went with carrying his title.

"The queen is not pleased," Montgomery went on.

Dorian's eyes snapped open, and he looked hard at Montgomery. "My mother has seen the pictures?"

"Yes."

That was all he needed. He had briefly spoken with her en route from Arlington to the military hospital and she'd been pleased with the press reports up to that point.

"So, what if Emmie was in some of the pictures? She's Gatsby's handler. I'm sure Brody and Chet have been in photos as well." He ran his hands through his hair then rested his palms on the back of the chair. "I don't understand what the big deal is. She works for me."

Montgomery's eyebrows raised momentarily. He reached into his pocket and pulled out his phone, his fingers swiping the screen. "Apparently, the photo your mother saw implies that Miss Walker is not merely an employee."

Dorian took the phone out of Montgomery's hand and stared at the screen. The photographer had captured the moment when Emmie was handing Dorian Gatsby's leash. They were gazing into each other's eyes with a look that implied much more than a work relationship. Dorian used his fingers to make the image larger, trying to read the expression on Emmie's face. *Could she have feelings for him?* His pulse quickened. A small smile formed on his lips. He studied the picture closer. Her eyes were focused on him as if there was no one else in the room. Her cheeks looked slightly flushed, her full lips slightly parted, and for one mad moment he wondered what it would be like to kiss them.

Montgomery cleared his throat and Dorian quickly buried his feelings of elation. With utmost seriousness, he handed Montgomery the phone and walked back to the window. His emotions were all over the place. On one hand, he understood what kind of media speculation that photo could cause. But on the other hand, the look he saw between him and Emmie in that photo made his heart race. He shouldn't think of her that way, he knew it, but he couldn't get her off his mind. She was enchanting.

"It's one photo, Montgomery. Don't make more out of it than it is. She's Gatsby's handler. It's perfectly acceptable for her to be around me in public." He wasn't sure if he was trying to convince himself or Montgomery.

"Of course, Your Highness," Montgomery said from behind him. They stood at the window and silently watched the scene below. Emmie knelt in the grass, and it appeared as though she was trying to teach Gatsby some sort of new trick. She lifted her head and laughed at something Trevor said. Dorian narrowed his eyes and his stomach tightened with a twinge of wariness. Trevor had worked with Dorian for a few years and Dorian trusted him implicitly. However, he did not care for the way he was looking at, or interacting with Emmie.

"I want Trevor reassigned," Dorian told Montgomery. "Put him on my detail. Put Chet with Gatsby." Chet had been with Dorian nearly as long as Montgomery had, was married and in his late fifties. Even to his own ears, Dorian realized how petty his request sounded. He'd never been much of a jealous man, but Emmie was bringing out feelings in him he'd never before experienced, and he didn't know how else to handle it.

"As you wish Your Highness," Montgomery said, with a slightly amused tone in his voice.

They stared silently for another moment at the scene playing out in the courtyard.

"She's quite a unique woman, Miss Walker," Montgomery murmured.

Dorian studied the man standing next to him as Montgomery focused on the activity on the other side of the window, his features softening in an almost melancholic expression. She even had Montgomery under her spell. Dorian returned his attention outside. Gatsby was running in circles around Emmie's feet, a joyous expression on both their faces.

"Yes, she is," Dorian agreed. *Yes, she is.*

EMMIE SAT ON THE bed in her room, studying the new itinerary. Kate had pressed it into her hands when she'd returned from working with Gatsby in the courtyard. They would be flying to Memphis on a charter plane that evening, and Dorian would take Gatsby, and her, to the Children's Hospital in the morning. A visit to a place called Troop Packs was scheduled for the following day and then they would fly on to Los Angeles for two nights for the big rescue gala with one final stop in San Francisco before the tour was over. Gatsby was now scheduled to accompany Dorian on each stop, which meant Emmie would be spending a considerable amount of time with him. A warmth spread across her body at the prospect.

She reached for her phone and tapped in the number of her grandmother's hospital room. She had tried to call earlier, but Agnes had answered and informed her that Blanche was sleeping. There hadn't been any change in her condition since Emmie had spoken with her the day before and it sounded like she was spending a great deal of time sleeping, largely due to the medications they were giving her for pain. The phone rang several times before Emmie heard the sound of it being picked up on the other end.

"Hello?" her grandmother answered, her voice sounding tired and raspy.

"Nana, it's Emmie. How are you?" Emmie slid back on the bed, leaned back against the pillows, and crossed her ankles.

"Emmie! I was hoping you'd call. I want to hear more about your prince."

"He's not my prince, Nana," Emmie said softly. "I want to hear how you are doing."

"I'm laid up in this insufferable hospital, what's there to say? I missed my bridge game today, and they are feeding me cardboard."

Emmie chuckled, "Nana, I'm sure they aren't feeding you cardboard."

"They might as well be," the old woman huffed, then coughed. Emmie heard rustling on the other end of the line and muffled voices. "Confounded nurses." Her voice came back on the line. "In and out all day long. If I charged admission, I'd be a rich woman by now."

Emmie sighed with relief. She was sounding more like her old self. While the words coming out of her mouth might sound cantankerous to a stranger's ear, Emmie knew it was just her way. Her grandmother was one of the most selfless, caring people she'd ever known.

"Are you feeling any better?"

"They got me taking these pills to help with the pains. Make me feel like I'm back in the 60s. I think they called it feeling spacey," she cackled.

Emmie smiled, "Is it helping though?"

"Yes, some. I told that new doctor he was going to turn me into a crazed addict, but he said I shouldn't worry about that. Do you think I need to worry about that, Emmie?"

Emmie could hear the concern in her grandmother's voice and feelings of homesickness and guilt for not being there washed over her. She reached for one of the pillows and hugged it to her chest. "No, Nana. You don't need to worry about that. Listen to them and take whatever they want you to take. They just want to make you feel better."

"They want all my money is what they want."

"Don't worry about that. You just worry about getting better."

"Tell me about your prince, I saw you making googly eyes at each other on the TV."

Emmie's breath caught in her throat, and she blinked. "What?"

"Agnes showed me. He's hot to trot, honey. I would make googly eyes at him too if I was you."

"Nana. I don't know what you saw, but I was *not* making googly eyes at him." *What was she talking about?*

"I know googly eyes when I see them," her grandmother insisted. "The TV people said he was at this fancy hospital, and they showed a picture of the two of you. They said they didn't know who you were, but I did. I yelled so loud I had all the nurses running in here like the place was on fire." She giggled, "I told them my granddaughter was bein' courted by royalty, but they patted my hand and told me to rest, like I was senile."

Oh no. She was supposed to stay away from the media. She couldn't afford to lose this job. She needed the money for her grandmother's hospital bills. Emmie closed her eyes and pinched the bridge of her nose.

"I'm not being courted by him," she finally said. "He wanted me to take the dog to the hospital to visit with the soldiers. My job is to take care of the dog. That's all."

"I may be old, Emmie, but I'm not blind. That prince is, how do you say it? Into you." She sounded pleased with herself.

Emmie was silent. *He couldn't possibly be interested in her, could he?* It didn't matter. He was royalty. She wasn't, and furthermore, he was her boss.

"Emmie? Are you there? Talk to me."

Emmie let out a long sigh, "Nana, it's not like...It can't be like that."

"Why can't it, honey? The heart doesn't care about titles."

"The heart might not, but the queen does. Besides, it's not like that," she reiterated.

"Are you trying to convince me or yourself?"

"That's enough of that now, Nana," Emmie chided, and changed the subject. "We're leaving for Memphis in a couple of hours."

"Memphis? You gonna see Elvis? I got to see him when I was your age. He was dreamy."

"No, I don't think we will have time to see Elvis," she said, trying to humor her grandmother. "If I do, I'll make sure to tell him hello from you though."

They laughed and her grandmother started coughing again. Emmie's heart sank to her toes as worry surged up and twisted around her heart. The care team was doing all they could for her, she just needed to trust it would be enough, but she couldn't help asking. "Nana, are you going to be okay?"

There was a long pause on the other end and Emmie pulled the phone from her ear to check if she was still connected. She was.

"Nana?" she prompted.

"I don't think so."

Emmie's shoulders slumped and she hugged the pillow tighter. The room blurred as tears filled her eyes. Her grandmother was the only person, only family, she had left in the world, and while Emmie knew she'd be gone at some point, she wasn't ready to lose her yet. She needed to be there with her.

"I'll catch the first flight to Minnesota I can get. I'm coming to be with you."

"You will do no such thing, missy. You will stay right there and finish your job."

"But—" Emmie began.

"But nothing. You will never get this chance again, Emmie. No sense in you sitting here so you can watch me sleep. You stay and be there for your prince. I will be just fine here."

Tears streamed down Emmie's face. "I can't let you be there all alone, Nana. I need you."

"I'm not alone, there are nurses in here all day long. And besides, Agnes has practically moved in. They even set up one of them reclining chairs for her to nap in. She snores like a congested moose."

Emmie laughed through her tears. "I'm sure it's not that bad."

"You have no idea." Her voice softened, "I'm fine Emmie. You need to stay there. Promise me."

Emmie let out a long breath, "Okay. I promise."

They said their I love you's and Emmie disconnected the call. The door to her room opened just a few inches and the shuffle of small feet sounded on the carpet. She peered over the edge of the bed and met Gatsby's gaze. She scooped up the corgi, hugged him close to her and let the tears fall.

CHAPTER 9

THE FLIGHT TO MEMPHIS was short and uneventful. Dorian appreciated being able to take the smaller charter jet rather than flying commercial for that hop. He'd spent most of the flight going over the new itinerary with Kate and Montgomery. There were a number of changes, and Kate insisted they run through it one more time.

He'd glanced back several times to where Emmie sat next to Gatsby. She'd had her eyes closed, although he didn't think she was sleeping. She'd been unusually quiet and subdued since their return from the military hospital and he couldn't help but wonder if something was wrong.

In the limo on the way to the hotel, Dorian attempted to make small talk with her, but Emmie's answers were short and flat. There was a sadness in her eyes that hadn't been there before, she sat quietly, her hands folded in her lap. There was now no doubt in Dorian's mind that something was bothering her. Once they checked in, Emmie headed directly to her assigned room and closed the door behind her. Gatsby looked up at Dorian, a confused expression on his face. Not knowing what to say to the perplexed animal, Dorian shrugged his shoulders. "I don't know either, buddy. We should probably give her some space." He cast an uneasy glance at her door and then went to familiarize himself with the suite.

The set-up here was different from the townhouse they'd had in Washington. This suite took up one whole corner of the floor of the hotel. It contained two living room areas with a full kitchen and formal dining room between them. Three bedrooms were situated off each living room with Kate, Montgomery and Brody on one side and Trevor, Chet and Emmie with him on the other. There were two beds in the room Trevor and Chet would share and the other rooms all contained king size beds. Each room had its own private bath. It wasn't the luxury he was used to at Dorburn, but it was comfortable.

The weather in Memphis was warm and muggy, unseasonably warm for springtime. Dorian poured himself a glass of wine and settled on the plush sofa in the living room on his side of the suite. He flipped aimlessly through the channels on the large television with Gatsby curled up next to him. He didn't have down time very often and was trying his best to relax and not worry about Emmie. She had yet to emerge from her room. The local news channel indicated there was a chance of severe weather during the night with strong thunderstorms likely. He got to his feet and padded to the window, pulling the heavy damask drapes aside to stare out into the inky night.

The bright lights of the Memphis nighttime skyline went on as far Dorian could see. He'd been to the United States before but had never really noticed how large the cities were. They stretched for miles. Avington was the only city on the Island of Avington, and you could see the clear waters of the North Sea on each side of it. From the castle windows you could see the entire island. He'd always thought of Avington as the semicolon of the North Sea, the city being the comma part and Dorburn Castle the dot above it.

As he stared at the cityscape, the events of the day ran through his mind. While he was enjoying his trip thus far, Dorian was already anxious to return home to work on some of the ideas he'd come up with while visiting the hospital. Avington had no need for a high-tech military hospital, but there was a need for a program to help veterans and their families.

One of the veterans he'd met that day was Randy, a young man who had lost his legs when his buddy stepped on a landmine. His friend lost his life, and Randy's legs were injured and damaged so badly with shrapnel they'd had to be amputated. He'd shared how he'd lost all faith and prayed every day for death to come release him from his misery. Randy had been a football player in high school, and he couldn't stand the thought of being in a wheelchair the rest of his life. Then his physical therapist told him about adaptive sports. He joined an adaptive rugby team and it changed not only his life, but his attitude about life. Randy was now not only an adaptive rugby coach, but he also went to hospitals around the country to give motivational talks to amputees.

Dorian, working with Montgomery, had already made appointments with the hospital and rehab facility in Avington to begin work on a charity he hoped to start that would have adaptive sports, among other services, to help veterans, whether injured or not. Serving in Afghanistan, alongside military soldiers from several different countries, had really opened Dorian's eyes to the plight of soldiers and the difficulties they faced when they returned home. He'd been lucky and he knew it. Now it was time for him to help those that weren't quite so lucky.

A flash of light caught his eye and Dorian returned his focus to the night sky. In the distance, thin fingers of lightning danced across the horizon. There was definitely something moving in. He made his way back to the sofa and stretched out his legs. Gatsby was lying on his back with his legs all akimbo on the far end of the sofa, snoring as if he didn't have a care in the world. Sometimes Dorian envied the dog's ability to roll with whatever came his way.

Unable to find anything he was interested in watching, Dorian clicked the television off and decided to head to his room. He paused at Emmie's door wondering if he should check on her. *What if she was sleeping?* He wouldn't want to wake her, but he was concerned. He'd only known her for a few days, but she somehow inconveniently managed to work her way into his life—and into his heart. Inconvenient because as a citizen, she was someone he knew he couldn't have. But, she was so different from any other woman he'd ever met. She was so natural, so authentic. She made him feel...like his title didn't matter. He lifted his hand to knock on the door, then slowly lowered it to his side. He'd let her rest and talk to her in the morning.

Something cold and wet was pushing against his cheek. Dorian tried to swat it away, but it came back, pushing harder. He rubbed his eyes, trying to get them to focus on the clock. The numbers read 2:15 a.m. *What is going on?*

Dorian sat up, shaking loose the sleep-woven cobwebs from his brain, and looked around. Flashes of light illuminated the room and he saw Gatsby standing next to him on the bed. It was Gatsby's nose he'd felt on his cheek. Thunder boomed and rain pelted the window.

"What's wrong, buddy? Are you scared?" he asked the dog. Gatsby wasn't typically afraid of storms, but he was pacing, running from Dorian to the edge of the bed and back. "Come on, let's go back to sleep. We have a busy day tomorrow." Dorian lay back down and patted the comforter next to him. Gatsby shoved his nose into his cheek again, this time adding a whine, clearly trying to tell him something. Dorian sat up and slid out of bed. He lifted Gatsby off the bed and set him on the floor. The dog's feet had barely touched the carpet when he ran to the door, scratching at it furiously.

Perplexed by the dog's antics, Dorian pulled it open. Gatsby ran through it like his tail was on fire and made a beeline straight for Emmie's door. He began scratching and whining with an intensity Dorian had never seen from the small dog. *Had something happened to Emmie?* His heart raced as he rushed across the room. He rapped on her door with his knuckles. "Emmie?" he called but got no reply. A bolt of lightning lit up the sky through the window and filled the room with a blinding flash of light, followed instantly by a tremendous crash of thunder. He thought he heard a sound from the other side of the door. Gatsby began howling and Dorian jiggled the doorknob. It wasn't locked.

He flung open the door. The bed was empty, but the lights in the bathroom were off. *Where was Emmie?* Another flash of lightning illuminated the room just enough for Dorian to see Gatsby dash along the side of the bed, the side farthest from the window.

Emmie was sitting on the floor, huddled up against the side table. Her knees were pulled tight to her chest, her forehead pressed against them, her hands pressed tightly over her ears. She rocked back and forth, her breath coming in stuttering gasps. She was having a panic attack. He'd seen it in the field in Afghanistan. Something had triggered this reaction and he'd find out what later, right now he needed to focus on calming her. Dorian rushed to kneel on the carpet next to Emmie, gathering her in his arms. A high-pitched noise came from her throat.

He shifted into a seated position, his legs on either side of her, and pulled her onto his lap, holding her close to his chest. Emmie threw her arms around him and buried her face in his neck, her whole body wracked with sobs. He rubbed her back in a circular motion and rocked with her.

"It's okay," he whispered against her ear. "Just breathe." He continued to rub her back and whisper soothing words until the storm raging outside, as well as the one raging inside her, subsided and she relaxed against him. Now only a light pattering of rain sounded against the window. Gatsby sat next to Dorian, watching Emmie closely. He'd have to remember to give the dog extra treats in the morning.

"Everything will be okay, Emmie," he murmured into her hair. The scent of it was an intoxicating blend of patchouli and berries. He could inhale the aroma forever and not tire of it. Something new and strange flooded through him. His title taught him not to let anyone get too close, but she made him laugh more and feel more...she made him want to risk it all.

"Th--th--they didn't come back. They said to stay put and they would be right back," she sobbed. "They never came back." Emmie let out a low, keening wail and pressed her cheek to his chest. He could feel her tears through his T-shirt. Whoever 'they' were, their disappearance clearly devastated her. Dorian continued to murmur comforting words into her hair and tried to calm her ragged breathing.

"Breathe, Emmie," he softly encouraged. "Take a deep breath. Come on, Emmie, breathe with me. Let's breathe in...two ...three ...four and then out...two ...three ...four." Dorian repeated this calming mantra several times until Emmie was breathing more normally, with just an occasional hitch. He cupped her face with his hand and gently raised her head so he could look at her. Her eyes were swollen and red from crying and she wouldn't meet his gaze.

"Emmie," he whispered. "Look at me."

He could sense the reluctance in her, but she slowly lifted her head until her beautiful eyes met his. Dorian didn't think he'd ever seen anyone look so despondent.

"Talk to me, Emmie," he murmured. He continued to stroke her hair and gently rocked her back and forth in what he hoped was a soothing motion.

"I'm so sorry Dorian," Emmie finally whispered. "The-the storm came up so fast and it was so loud."

"It's okay. It's past us now," Dorian replied in a soothing voice.

"It was just like that night—" Her breath hitched, and tears once again began streaming down her face.

Dorian knew it would be difficult for Emmie to talk about whatever happened that night, but he also knew it would be therapeutic. "What night? Tell me about it," he encouraged her in a soft voice.

Emmie took a deep, ragged breath and let it out slowly. "I was twelve," she began, her voice flat and tired. "We'd all gone to bed and sometime during the night, the storm sirens went off. We didn't have a basement. It was so loud, it sounded like the train jumped the tracks and was running right beside the house. Dad told me to go lie in the bathtub. He and mom went to get a mattress to cover it. They said they'd be right back. The tornado hit the house before they had a chance to return. They-they were both killed."

Dorian drew her in closer and held her tightly. He knew all too well the pain of losing a parent at a young age, but he couldn't imagine what it must have been like for her to lose them both at the same time and so violently.

"I'm so sorry, Em," he whispered in her ear, fighting the urge to kiss her.

"When it storms really hard like this, it freaks me out," she said. "I usually pay very close attention to the weather. I have a pill I can take, but I was distracted when we got here and forgot to check."

Emmie settled against his chest and yawned deeply. Dorian wanted to ask more about her parents and what had distracted her earlier in the evening, but he could see her eyelids were heavy.

"It was quite a storm," he agreed. "Let's get you into bed now so you can rest." He helped her to stand, then rose to his feet. He slid one arm under her knees and the other under her shoulders and lifted her; she looped her arms around his neck and held on tight. He laid her gently on the bed and tucked the covers around her. Then he bent and picked up Gatsby, placing him next to her.

"Gatsby will stay with you the remainder of the night," he murmured, running his finger along her soft cheek.

Emmie reached up and clutched Dorian's hand. "Thank you, Dorian," she said, her voice thick and raspy with sleep, her eyelids heavy.

Dorian fought the urge to kiss her. He'd wait until she was feeling better so when he did – and there would be a when – he'd know she was kissing him back because she meant it. He was a gentleman, and a gentleman wouldn't take advantage of her in her present state. He ran a thumb along her jaw instead. "Good night sweet Emmie," he whispered.

CHAPTER 10

Emmie awoke to the sound of snoring. Confused, she reached behind her and felt along the comforter until her fingers connected with soft fur. Gatsby. What was he doing there? She rolled over and stretched, then ran her fingers through the dog's silky pelt. He lay on his back, all four feet straight up in the air, snoring contentedly. The memory of the night before washed over her like a bad dream. The entire scene unfolded in her mind, making her stomach twist. She lifted her hands, her face hot under her palms. Not only had she consorted with the Prince, *during the night*, she'd had a complete meltdown in his arms. His arms around her had felt so good though, strong and safe. She rubbed the sleep from her eyes and slipped out of bed.

The aroma of fresh brewed coffee wafted through the air, beckoning her. She pulled her hair up into a messy bun and slid her feet into her favorite pair of scuffs. She needed coffee. She *wanted* ice cream. She always did when her world went pear-shaped, but coffee would have to do this morning. Deciding to let the snoring corgi rest, Emmie shuffled toward the kitchen. Gatsby could sleep through just about anything!

She stopped short when she saw Dorian perched on a stool at the counter. Heat crept into her cheeks. A steaming mug sat on the counter in front of him and he was paging through the local newspaper. He wore a light grey suit with a light blue shirt and no tie. It was nice to see him semi-casual for a change, even if the suit was designer. Kate was also in the kitchen making tea, and Emmie tried to avoid eye contact with the woman as she pulled a mug down and filled it with brew.

"Good morning, Emmie. I hope you slept well." Dorian greeted her with a warm smile and subtle wink. Relief coursed through her, and she gave him a grateful smile in return.

"The storm kept me up, but I'm fine this morning." Emmie settled onto the tall stool next to him. She hooked her feet around the stool's legs, and twirled a stray lock of hair with her fingers. She gave Dorian a meaningful smile. "Thank you," she whispered and found herself unable to look away.

"Emmie," Kate's sharp voice snapped Emmie from her inappropriate ogling. "You and Gatsby will be traveling to the hospital with Chet. His Highness and I will meet you there promptly at ten o'clock." She regarded Emmie's tousled hair and rumpled pajamas with disdain and raised an eyebrow. "I trust you will be ready by then?"

Emmie bit back the sarcastic response that sprang to her lips. She knew she needed to tread carefully, she needed this job.

"Of course, Ms. Baker." Emmie gave Kate a broad grin. "I'll be ready. I can't say when Gatsby will wake up, but we'll do our best to be on time." Dorian chuckled softly beside her. Kate's eyes grew wide for a second, then narrowed.

"See that you both are," Kate replied with a tense sniff.

Brody entered the kitchen and announced the car was ready to take Dorian to his breakfast meeting with the Memphis Paralympic Committee. Dorian rose, stretched his long arms over his head, and tried to stifle a yawn. A pang of guilt swept through Emmie. She knew he was tired because of her. She shot him an apologetic look and her lips pulled back in a slight grimace. He picked up his coffee mug and carried it to the sink, his mouth upturned in an easy smile. On his way past, Dorian paused, placed a hand on the back of the stool where she sat, and leaned toward her.

"I'm glad you're okay. Let's talk more about it later," he murmured, his warm breath tickling her ear.

Emmie nodded in agreement, words failing to form in her mind, let alone her mouth. Dorian straightened and strode to the door. He stopped at the threshold and turned back. "Your hair is cute like that." He winked and pulled the door shut behind him.

Did he just wink at me? Emmie's whole body tingled at the thought, but she pushed it away. He could have anyone he wanted. There was no way he'd pick someone like her—a plus size, soon-to-be-unemployed dog trainer who lived with her grandmother and was afraid of thunderstorms. Emmie snorted at the idea, then remembered her grandmother saying something about a photo of her and Dorian while they were talking the night before.

She slid off the stool and darted into her room, grabbing her phone off the nightstand. Gatsby was still snoring. She gingerly perched on the edge of the bed so she wouldn't wake him. Emmie swiped the screen and put Dorian's name in the search engine. A second later, the screen was filled with images of the prince. Several included her. She used her fingers to enlarge the one where the photographer had captured her handing Dorian Gatsby's leash and couldn't help gaping at it. Nana was right. *Googly eyes.*

EMMIE CLIMBED OUT OF the limo, secured Gatsby, and walked with Chet through the entrance of the Children's Hospital. An anxious woman in a dark blue suit greeted them. Her eyes were bright, and her face flushed as she shook their hands and told them to follow her. She explained the prince was in the family resource center and tittered about how wonderful it was to have a real live prince visiting the kids.

The hallways were unlike any hospital Emmie had been in, and she'd spent a fair amount of time in hospitals. The walls were painted to look like rolling hills dotted with trees and flowers and the ceiling above like the sky, in a brilliant, bright blue. Another hallway was done in a space mural, with stars, planets and the moon scattered across a dark, celestial background. They followed the woman through a maze of theme-painted hallways to the resource center.

This room was huge and reminded Emmie of a library designed specifically for children. Brightly colored chairs and bean bags were situated in various groupings throughout the room. Short bookshelves painted in primary colors lined with books, magazines and DVDs. A peal of laughter drew her attention to a reading area where a large crowd of children gathered around Dorian. They were dressed in colorful pajamas and many clung to their favorite stuffed animals. Emotion pricked the backs of Emmie's eyes as she noted several of them also had IV stands next to them.

"It's a puppy," a towheaded little girl cried. She squealed as she ran toward Emmie and Gatsby. Dorian looked up from the book he was reading and gave Emmie a warm smile before returning to his story. Emmie crouched beside Gatsby and helped the girl gently pet the dog. Soon there were so many fingers reaching for Gatsby, Emmie was forced to pull him back. She put her hands up, effectively blocking the onslaught of little hands.

"Hey kids, you know how you feel when lots of nurses and doctors come into your room all at the same time?" she asked the children.

"Yes," a young boy replied. "It's scary."

"I feel like something bad is gonna happen," chimed another child.

"Okay. Well, Gatsby feels the same way when all of you want to pet him at once," Emmie told them.

"Oh no, we don't want to scare him," cried a little girl.

"If you come up one at a time and pet him nice and slow, he won't be scared anymore," Emmie assured them and watched with wide eyes as the children organized themselves into a line in order to pet the dog. Gatsby was loving the attention and even rolled on his back to get some belly rubs, which elicited more squeals of laughter from the children.

Dorian, finished with his book, strolled over, and stood next to Emmie. He placed his hand on her shoulder, then, as if he realized where he'd placed it, pulled it back and slid it into his pants pocket. The heat from his hand radiated through her shirt and sent butterflies through her stomach.

Emmie caught Kate's disapproving glare and took a step to the side, widening the gap between her and Dorian. He gave her a quizzical look and a rush of heat flooded her cheeks. Watching him interact on such a genuine level with the children only made fighting her attraction to him that much more difficult.

She caught the amusement in his eyes as he stepped forward, closing the space she'd just made between them. She could smell the clean, spicy scent of his aftershave and her stomach plunged. He flashed her a mischievous smile before crouching next to Gatsby and turning his attention back to the children gathered around them.

"Did you know that Gatsby is royalty too?" He fluffed the fur on Gatsby's neck and patted the dog on his back.

"He is?" asked one child, his voice full of skepticism.

"How can a dog be royal?" asked another.

"Is he a king?" a small voice wondered.

"He's a duke," Dorian informed the children.

"A duke, like in the song?" asked a boy.

"Yes!" Dorian beamed. "Only Gatsby is the Duke of Fluffington."

The children giggled hysterically, as did some of the medical staff and Emmie found herself drawn into the merriment.

"Who knows the Duke song?" Dorian asked the children, rising to his feet. Nearly all their hands went up. "All right, let's sing it about Gatsby! Let's all find a chair." He waited while the kids scrambled to fill the small chairs that had been arranged in a large semi-circle.

"Now, when I say 'up' you stand, and when I say 'down' you sit back down. Does everyone understand?"

"Yes!" the children cheered. Emmie thought her heart would melt right out of her chest as she watched him lead the kids in song.

"Oh, the grand old Duke of Fluffington," Dorian sang in a deep baritone voice, the children joining in. "He had ten thousand men, he marched them *up* to the top of—" he gestured with his arms for everyone to stand up and continued with the verse "—the hill and he marched them *down* again." He then motioned for everyone to sit. "And when they were *up,* they were *up.* —" Again, he motioned for the children to stand, most of them were laughing so hard they had a hard time getting back on their feet. "And when they were *down*, they were *down.*" The children fell to the floor in hysterics. "And when they were only halfway *up*, they were neither *up* nor *down.*"

By the time they were done, the kids were worn out from the exertion of the song and the fun they were having. Emmie noticed that even Kate was unable to suppress a grin.

"Great job, you guys," Dorian applauded them. "That was the best song I ever heard."

The kids all cheered and clapped.

"Are you Pwince Ewic from the Wittle Mermaid?" A young girl, about four years old, asked Dorian. She was tiny and frail, with dark shadows beneath her large brown eyes. Emmie glanced at Dorian. With his dark wavy hair, strong jaw, and white shirt, he totally looked the part.

Dorian laughed. "No, I'm still looking for my Ariel." He slid a quick glance to Emmie, and a shiver raced down her spine.

Dorian talked with the children, stooping down so he was at eye-level with them. He listened carefully to each one as they told him stories about their families, their illnesses, and their dreams. He gave them hugs and high fives, and Emmie's heart tumbled in her chest.

"You have a scar too?" A small voice pulled Emmie's attention away from Dorian. A young girl that looked to be about seven years old stood next to her. She had wide blue eyes set in the cutest pixie face. She clutched an IV pole in one hand and a teddy bear with a bright red ribbon carefully tied around its neck in the other. One half of her head had short, light brown hair and the other was shaved with two puckered cuts on her scalp held together with dark stitches.

Emmie lifted her hand and ran her fingers along the scar that began on the bottom of her chin. She didn't care to talk about her scars, even though she knew people looked and wondered, but this was different. This little girl wasn't looking at her with pity.

"Yes, I do."

"My name is Daisy," the girl said shyly, holding her bear close.

"Hi Daisy," Emmie replied. "My name is Emmie. Did you know daisies are my favorite flower?"

Daisy's face lit up, "Really?"

"Really, truly," Emmie smiled. "And who is this?" She gestured to the bear.

"Charlie."

Emmie shook the bear's paw. "Nice to meet you too, Charlie."

Daisy gave her a shy smile. "My scar is because I had to have surgery on my brains. Did you have to have surgery on your face?"

"No, I didn't have surgery. Mine are from a tornado."

"Like the Wizard of Oz?"

"Kind of. Only there weren't any wicked witches."

"How did the tornado hurt your face?" Daisy stepped closer, studying Emmie's scar closely.

"Well, when a tornado comes, it gets really windy, and that makes all kinds of things fly around. Some of those things hit me on my face and my arm," Emmie pulled the sleeve up on her left arm revealing a long, twisted rope scar similar to the one that traveled up her left leg. The left side of her torso was lined with them too. "I have some on my leg and back too."

Daisy reached a tentative hand forward and gently ran her finger along the scar on Emmie's arm. "Wow. That must have hurt really bad," she said, gazing into Emmie's eyes. "I just have scars on my head, but they don't hurt very much. Mommy says my hair will cover them up, but yours can't cover up, can they?"

Emmie stared past the girl, focusing on an empty space in the air between them. Her mind went back to her high school prom. She'd finally gotten the nerve to ask Tommy Jenkins to take her. Tommy sat in front of her in her history class and she'd had a crush on him all year. When she asked, he'd laughed in her face and told her he wasn't going to a dance with a scarred-up freak. She spent that night eating ice cream with her grandmother and vowed that she'd never let anything like that happen to her again. Never put herself in position to be ridiculed like that. Emmie returned her attention to Daisy.

"No, they can't cover up," she said in a low voice. She was glad Daisy's hair would cover her scars so she wouldn't have to go through that kind of humiliation.

"Well, I think you're still really pretty! Don't you, Prince Dorian?" Daisy inquired.

Emmie stiffened and slowly turned her head, meeting Dorian's gaze. He'd been listening. She saw affection in his eyes and a smile tugged at his lips.

"Yes," he said in a low voice. "I think she's beautiful."

If Emmie hadn't already been kneeling by Gatsby, her knees would have buckled. Her breath caught and her gaze lingered on his. *He thinks I'm beautiful?*

"Is she your girlfriend?" A voice piped up behind them.

"Are you a princess?" another voice asked.

Oh no! Emmie's gaze broke from Dorian and met a sea of young faces, eagerly waiting for answers. A flash of heat ran up her neck into her face and ears.

"N-no, I'm not a princess," she stammered, wishing she could disappear.

Dorian raised his arm, signaling to Kate who stood near the reception table, a dour expression on her face. She gave a curt nod in return and rushed off with Brody and Chet. They returned a moment later, Brody and Chet's arms loaded with shopping bags. Dorian reached into one of the bags and pulled out a tiara, carefully placing it on the head of the girl who had asked if Emmie was a princess.

"I think *you're* a princess," Dorian told the child, smiling so widely his eyes crinkled in the corners. "I think you can all be a princess, or ball players, or scientists, or anything you want." He opened the bags, and they were filled with tiaras, balls and gloves, toy trucks, and dolls. The children squealed with excitement as they rushed to choose a treasure.

Emmie had to fight to keep tears from welling up in her eyes. What an extraordinary thing for him to do. Dorian rose to his feet and stepped aside to allow the children better access to their gifts.

They said their goodbyes and were walking toward the door when Emmie heard a little voice call her name. She turned and saw Daisy walking toward her, Charlie bear and a new doll under one arm and the other awkwardly pulling the IV pole with her.

"Wait, Miss Emmie, wait," Daisy called.

Emmie stopped and crouched down next to Daisy. "What is it, Daisy?"

Daisy thrust her teddy bear into Emmie's arms, "I want you to have Charlie."

Emmie's mouth opened, then closed, her heart melting. "Daisy honey, I can't take your bear."

"But you need him, Miss Emmie. Charlie makes me feel better when I get sad about my scars," Daisy pushed the bear into Emmie's hands and held up her new doll. "Prince Dorian gave me this new doll. Isn't she pretty?"

"She is very pretty," Emmie agreed. She could feel the tears begin to pool in her eyes.

"She can make me feel better about my scars now, and you can have Charlie to make you feel better about yours," Daisy explained.

"Thank you, Daisy, that's very sweet of you. I promise I'll take good care of Charlie for you. What are you going to name your new doll?"

"Emmie, because she is brave like you."

"Thank you, Daisy," Emmie sniffled. "Always be brave, sweet girl." Emmie gave Daisy another hug then rose and walked back to where Dorian and Gatsby waited, swiping the tears from her eyes, and holding Charlie bear close. The simple gesture was the purest form of kindness she'd ever seen and she struggled to hold herself together.

As they walked through the maze of halls toward the entrance, Dorian slowed his gait so he could match Emmie's steps. He hesitated before reaching to brush a hand down her arm in a small gesture of comfort. "Are you okay?" he whispered.

Emmie opened her mouth to speak, but Kate cut her off.

"Miss Walker, I think you've said quite enough today." She scowled at Emmie before turning her attention to Dorian. "Your Highness, the press will be in the atrium, and we must not have another incident like the one at the Veterans Hospital."

CHAPTER 11

"THERE *WAS* NO INCIDENT at the Veterans Hospital," Dorian said in a low, controlled voice. He knew he'd opened a Pandora's Box when he insisted Gatsby accompany him on the remaining appearances, but he wanted to spend more time getting to know Emmie. It wasn't his fault the press had captured an innocent moment and turned it into something else. They did stuff like that all the time.

"The press is insinuating there was. After the accusations from Ms. Easton, I would think you'd be more mindful of whom you're consorting with."

Dorian took a deep breath, his patience worn thin. "Who I *consort* with is not your concern."

"Your Highness, she—"

"Enough," Dorian snapped, cutting her off. "We're not having this discussion here. Or anywhere. Emmie has done nothing wrong."

"You mean Miss Walker, don't you, Your Highness?" Kate corrected him with a disapproving frown.

Dorian stopped. Kate had worked for his family for more years than Dorian could remember, and he knew his mother regarded her highly, but he would not tolerate this behavior from her. From anyone.

"Be careful Ms. Baker," he warned. "Your job is much more on the line than hers right now."

"The queen has given me strict instructions with regard to Miss Walker."

"And you are here with *me*. Not the queen."

Kate pursed her lips and pressed a hand to her neck, but nodded in understanding.

Dorian turned to face Emmie. Her face was flushed, and she looked horrified. This had turned into a hot mess, but he was tired of catering to everyone else's whim and plan. *He* was a prince; he could make his own plans for once.

He grabbed Emmie's hand. "Come with me."

She blinked at him, her brow raised. "What?"

"Come with me," he repeated, gently tugging her hand. "Let's get out of here."

"I DON'T CARE," HE said and realized at that moment, he didn't. "Let's go." He flashed her a smile, his voice full of mischief, and grabbed Gatsby.

They managed to elude Dorian's bodyguards by slipping into a stairwell, and hopped into one of the many cabs parked in front of the hospital waiting for fares.

"Go! Just drive," Dorian told the driver, glancing over his shoulder to see if they were being followed. Not seeing anyone, he relaxed his shoulders and settled into the seat.

"I can't believe you just did that," Emmie said, out of breath from their run. "Kate's going to blow a gasket."

"Very likely," Dorian laughed. He hadn't felt this free since...since *ever*. He pulled Gatsby onto his lap and held his furry companion since he had no car seat. Now that they were away from the hospital, he had no idea what to do. He just knew he needed to get out of there. "I'm not sure where to go. I haven't got a plan."

"Do you plan everything?" Emmie asked.

"Yes, always. I can't remember the last time I didn't have an itinerary or schedule to follow."

"Go to Beale Street," Emmie told the driver, then turned her attention back to Dorian. "First thing we need to do," she said, studying his outfit, "is to get you out of those clothes."

Dorian's mouth formed an O.

Emmie's face pinked as she realized her error and she elbowed him in the ribs. "Not like *that*. We need to get you into something that doesn't scream 'I'm a prince," she said, making air quotes with her fingers.

He glanced down at his suit. "What's wrong with this? I'm not even wearing a tie."

Emmie shook her head, momentarily closing her eyes. "How long do you think it will take someone to recognize you in that? It's a Brioni. Us common folk don't wear Brioni suits." She wiggled her eyebrows at him. "We need to find you something that blends in better. Unless you prefer that we find you a crown and advertise who you are."

"You have a point," he conceded.

The cabbie dropped them off on Beale Street. Dorian held Gatsby close as he looked up and down the busy street. He'd never been without his bodyguards in public. As far as the eye could see, the busy street was lined with shops, and each seemed to have a neon sign hanging over its door. Crowds of people filled the sidewalks and Dorian could smell a unique blend of car exhaust, smoke, coffee, and fried food.

Emmie surveyed the stores around them. "This one is perfect." She tucked Charlie bear under her arm and motioned for Dorian to follow. She led him into a store called Thrifty Blues. It boasted having the best recycled and upcycled clothing in Memphis.

The store was huge. Racks upon racks of hanging clothes filled the center and shelves laden with shoes of every kind lined the walls. He watched Emmie rifling through the racks, pulling out a variety of T-shirts and jeans. He was used to a tailor showing him swatches of fabric and having a custom fit suit delivered to him at the castle a few weeks later. He'd never shopped off the rack before. Emmie thrust the hangers full of clothes at him.

"I'll take Gatsby. You go try these on. I think I got your size right," she said, taking Gatsby from him. She pointed to a small closet with a chipped louvered door marked *Dressing Room*.

Dorian looked at the assortment of jeans and shirts in his arms and was struck with a sudden realization. The clothes were used. Did people actually purchase *used* clothing? He glanced around the store at the multitude of shoppers perusing the racks. *When in Rome...*

Thirty minutes later, they emerged from the store. Much of that time was spent by Emmie convincing him that people not only wore 'recycled' clothes, but for many it was their preferred wardrobe. Decked out in a pair of Levi's jeans and a Nashville Predators T-shirt, Dorian experienced a deep, refreshing feeling of freedom. Emmie had tried talking him into getting a Graceland shirt, but he had to draw the line somewhere. Plus, he enjoyed watching American hockey. They'd found a pair of new loafers in his size and a new dark grey baseball cap. A pair of mirrored aviator sunglasses completed his ensemble. He felt more *normal* than he ever had in his life.

Emmie had even found an "Elvis Lives" shirt for Gatsby. She pulled her long, brown hair into a low ponytail at the nape of her neck and donned a new dark blue baseball cap. None of the women he knew would be caught dead in a baseball cap, but Emmie not only looked comfortable wearing it, she looked beautiful in it.

They strolled aimlessly down Beale Street, chatting about the different sights and sounds they encountered on the busy street. Dorian's expensive suit and loafers were stuffed in a bag he now carried on his wrist, Emmie's Charlie bear lying carefully on top. Dorian was enjoying the freedom of his new anonymity. While a few people did a double take, most walked past him without a second glance.

Emmie spied a pet store called Blues Collars and they went inside. Dorian rarely shopped in the private sector and was amazed at the variety of stores and merchandise. He enjoyed choosing a large selection of toys and clothes for Gatsby. He reached for a bag of treats and Emmie stopped him.

"Not those." She pulled them from his hand and hung them back up, selecting a different bag. "These are better for him."

"What was wrong with those?" Dorian's brows knit together. "They looked good." *What difference did it make? They were both liver flavored.*

"Yes, but the one you picked was liver *flavored* and full of fillers. This one is made with real liver and is all natural," she informed him. "Gatsby doesn't need fillers like ground corn. It will make him gassy."

Gatsby gazed up at Emmie and cocked his head, a disdainful expression on his furry face.

"I had no idea." Dorian rubbed his jaw and bent to scratch Gatsby's chin. "Sorry buddy," he said and rose back to his feet. "The food and treats are just there for him. I guess I don't think about where it comes from or what's in it. I trust Howard to take care of that."

"We've made a few adjustments, Howard and I," Emmie smiled. "Gatsby is now eating a slightly more balanced diet. What he was eating was fine, just a little protein-rich for his breed."

Dorian watched her select a few more treats for the dog before he paid for their purchases, and they left the store. He'd have to remember to thank Montgomery for hiring her. They approached a park and Dorian looked curiously at a row of brightly decorated trucks with what appeared to be service counters. *Were they serving food?*

Emmie squealed, gripping his upper arm and pointed to a bright yellow truck with fat letters spelling out Say Cheese. "They have grilled cheese!

I love grilled cheese." She looked at him, her eyes lit up like an excited child's.

"There? In that truck?" Dorian was confused. "How does one actually grill cheese?"

Emmie looked at him incredulously. "You've never had grilled cheese? I'd ask if you were born under a rock, but I suppose being born in a castle explains it. And yes, these are food trucks. They don't have them in Avington?"

Dorian shook his head, still trying to figure out exactly what a *grilled cheese* was. "No. To both, I'm afraid," he shrugged.

Emmie pointed to an empty bench on the other side of the sidewalk, "Go sit over there, I'll grab us a couple sandwiches." Dorian took Gatsby to the bench and sat, arranging their bags beside him. He studied Emmie as she stood in line. A month ago, if you'd have told him he would be sitting in used clothes waiting to eat cheese that was grilled without his bodyguards, he would have laughed. Now, it didn't seem so crazy.

Gatsby lay under the bench, gnawing happily on a chew bone Dorian had bought for him at the pet store. Emmie came back to the bench with two wrapped packages and two bottles of water. She sat beside him, taking the paper wrap off what appeared to be a sandwich consisting of noodles and a yellow/orange sauce between two thick slices of toasted bread. She handed it to him and began unwrapping hers. Steam rose from the sandwich and an aroma that he could only describe as an interesting combination of butter and cheddar cheese filled his nose.

"It's a Mac Daddy-O," Emmie explained. She took a bite out of her sandwich and her eyes closed. "Oh my gosh," she remarked with a groan. "This is *so good*."

Dorian looked at the sandwich in his hands with skepticism and stole a glance at Emmie. She was clearly enjoying hers.

"Just eat it, Dorian," she said with a taunting lilt in her voice and took another bite.

Here goes nothing. Dorian lifted the sandwich to his mouth and bit off a huge bite. The bread was crisp in contrast to the soft cheesy noodles and rich sauce. It was like nothing he'd ever tasted, and it was pure bliss.

"This is amazing, Em," he said around a mouthful of sandwich.

"If the press could see you now," she laughed. "Speaking of which, are you missing the three musketeers yet?"

"Who?"

"Trevor, Brody and Chet. I don't know how you can handle them breathing down your neck all the time, watching every move you make. It would drive me nuts."

Dorian had just taken another huge bite and almost choked on his sandwich. He'd never heard his bodyguards referred to as the three musketeers before and the reference made him want to laugh out loud. He swallowed and said with a chuckle, "I never thought about how strange that must be to you. For me, *this* is strange. I can't remember being out in public without bodyguards or staff." Dorian thought for a moment. "Ever."

Emmie lifted her brows at his response and wiped her mouth with a napkin. "That seems so weird to me. I guess I'm just used to being alone quite a bit. I mean, it's just me and my grandmother at the apartment. Plus, Bernie and I have been traveling so much, so it's not like I'm even really there very often."

Dorian's stomach fell. For some reason he hadn't considered she was in a relationship, but now he couldn't see why she wouldn't be in one. "Is Bernie your boyfriend?"

CHAPTER 12

Emmie threw her head back and burst into laughter. The look on Dorian's face made her laugh even harder and she had to focus on the food truck for a moment to regain her composure.

"I certainly hope not," she chuckled. "Bernie is a corgi. That's how I met Montgomery. He was at the Crestwood Hills Dog Show with Bernie's owner in New York. I worked and traveled with him for the past few years."

A mixture of relief and embarrassment crossed Dorian's face. "He said you were a dog handler but didn't mention the name of the dog you worked with. That also explains his recent trip to New York City. Are you not working with Bernie anymore?"

"He retired after Crestwood Hills."

"Are you going to miss it?"

"I'll miss Bernie, but not the dog show circuit. It's a lot more political than you'd think."

"I understand political," he gave a rueful laugh. "What will you do when you're done with me—I mean Gatsby?"

When she was done with him. She only had a few days before she was *done with him*, done with Gatsby. How could she have grown so attached so quickly? She gave herself a mental shake and cleared her throat. "I'd like to open a service dog training facility."

"That would be amazing, Emmie."

She gave a half smile. "It would. There are things that need to be taken care of first, though."

Dorian nodded and Emmie was grateful he didn't press her for more information. He leaned back against the bench and rubbed the slight scruff that was beginning to form on his jaw. "So, no boyfriend then?"

Emmie hesitated. Dorian dated movie stars and was considered a very eligible bachelor. He probably had loads of experience with women. She, on the other hand, had very little experience with men. She'd dated a little after high school, but nothing serious. "Well, Bernie tended to be jealous so...." She needed to change the subject fast. She took another bite of her sandwich and chewed thoughtfully. "You were wonderful with the kids this morning," she said, after she swallowed.

Dorian's face softened. "Thank you. I love kids. I spend as much time with my nephew Archer, as I can." He leaned forward and extended his hand toward her. "You have some cheese right—" his thumb brushed the corner of her mouth, lingering for just an instant "—there." They looked into each other's eyes for a long moment, before Dorian sat back.

"The girl you were talking to, what was her name—Daisy?"

It took Emmie a second to make sense of what he'd said. She could still feel the heat from his thumb on the corner of her mouth. She nodded, balling up her sandwich wrapper and tossing it into the garbage can next to the bench where they sat.

"She reminded me a lot of my sister Ava." Dorian looked down at his empty wrapper, picked at a bit of stray cheese that was stuck to it, then crumpled it up and threw it away.

"I didn't know you have a sister."

"I *had* a sister. Ava had leukemia and died when she was six."

Emmie put her hand on his arm. "I'm so sorry, Dorian."

He gave her a wistful smile, "It was a long time ago. But it's one of the reasons I try to spend time at the children's hospitals. I'm actually in the process of setting up a charity called Ava's Angels to help parents with sick children so they can afford to take time off work to care for their families without having to worry about bills."

"That's incredible, Dorian." Emmie couldn't imagine being in a position to help people like that.

Dorian gazed at her quietly for a moment, a quizzical expression on his face. Emmie could tell he wanted to ask her something, but he looked like he was debating whether or not he should.

She took a drink from her water bottle and bent over to check on Gatsby. He was in full corgi *sploot*, snoring contentedly. She turned her attention back to Dorian. "What?" she prompted.

Dorian rubbed the back of his neck and took a deep breath. "I heard what you said to Daisy. About how you got your scars. I was impressed with how open you were with her. Do they still bother you?"

Emmie thought about it for a few seconds. *Did they still bother her?* "I don't know," she said with a sigh. "Most of the time I don't think about them. When I let myself think about what caused them and what I lost that night, they do. I guess we all have scars though. Some are just on the inside." She took another sip of her water. "It bothers me when I wear clothes that allow them to show and people stare or, even worse, get that—that look, you know? Pity. It makes me uncomfortable. I don't like it."

"I get that. I don't like it either."

"You? Why would anyone look at you with pity?" she snorted. "You're a prince. You can have anything you want."

"It's really not like a fairytale, Emmie. My uncle, my dad's brother, used to look at me like that. He'd always refer to my brother Philip and me as 'the heir and the spare.' The media does it too. 'Philip is going to be king someday. What are *you* going to do, Dorian?'" He gave a rueful chuckle. "I have to worry about everyone's motives. Are they genuine or are they just looking for publicity?"

Emmie gazed into his eyes and saw a flash of pain. It must be awful to have to constantly wonder if people associated with you because they liked you or if it was only because of your title, or to constantly be compared to someone else. Suddenly, she didn't think being royal was such a grand thing.

"That would stink," she acknowledged.

His lips curled in a droll smile. "Sometimes. Most of the time it's worth it though. It opens a lot of doors."

"So, what *are* you going to do, Prince Dorian?"

Dorian stretched his long arms over his head, adjusted his ball cap and then clasped his hands around the knee of his crossed legs. Emmie thought he looked more relaxed than she'd ever seen him.

"Right now, I'm just a man with a dog sitting on a bench in a park, trying to get to know a girl."

Emmie gave him a playful shove. "I'll bet you say that to all the girls."

"You aren't like other girls, Em." He tucked a stray hair behind her ear. "You're not like anyone I've ever met." His voice was low and husky. He leaned closer, his gaze sliding from her eyes down to her lips.

All rational thought left Emmie's head. *Is he going to kiss me?* Her whole body began tingling like there was a low voltage current going through it. She gazed at his mouth and had the sudden urge to find out if his lips were as soft as they looked.

A blue Frisbee whizzed between them and hit the back of the bench with a loud thwack. It was so close, the air moved as it passed Emmie's face and she jerked her head back. Dorian shot to his feet, his jaw clenched tight as his eyes scanned the area.

"Are you okay?" he asked, his voice thick with concern.

Emmie swallowed hard. "I'm fine."

Gatsby began to bark, and Dorian bent to reassure the startled dog that everything was all right.

"Oh man, I'm sorry, dude." A teenage boy wearing shorts, flip flops, and a T-shirt emblazoned with the logo of some metal band Emmie had never heard of rushed up to the bench to retrieve the Frisbee. He ran a hand through his short, blond hair. "That was like, so cool though. It totally flew right between you guys."

"It wouldn't have been *cool* if it had hit her." Dorian handed the boy his Frisbee. "Be more careful with that."

"Lighten up, man," the teen retorted and ambled off toward his friends.

Dorian shook his head. "The—what did you call them? My bodyguards. The three musketeers? They would have laid that kid flat."

"Yeah, I guess I hadn't thought about how *you* feel without them close. Are you concerned?" Emmie glanced around, trying to see if anything looked suspicious. She was beginning to realize how vulnerable he was without the bodyguards nearby. "Maybe we should head back to the hotel. I'll get us a car." She pulled her phone out of her pocket to arrange for an Uber.

"It's all right, it was just a kid. I'll likely never have the opportunity to be untethered again after this," he chuckled. "Let's walk back. It's not that far. I think I remember seeing this park through the window at the hotel."

He gathered their shopping bags and Gatsby's leash. "You ready to go, buddy?" Gatsby looked at Dorian and wagged his tail, appearing to be in favor of that plan.

They walked the rest of the way down Beale Street in comfortable silence. People filled the sidewalks, going in and out of shops, bars, and restaurants. Emmie tried to convince herself that she had imagined that moment on the bench. He surely wouldn't want to kiss her. What was she thinking?

She was completely out of his league. In just a few days, he'd be going back to his castle in Europe, and she'd be going back to Minnesota.

They strolled past a Christmas-themed store that had a window display containing a huge selection of tree ornaments. A crystal cardinal ornament caught her attention and she stopped. Thoughts of her grandmother filled her head. She had an immense collection of cardinal figurines and ornaments. A lump formed in her throat and tears pricked the backs of her eyes.

Dorian lightly bumped her with his elbow. "You're so quiet. Are you okay?"

Emmie let out a sigh and looked down at her hands. She'd been rubbing the palm of one hand with the thumb of the other and didn't even realize it, a nervous habit she'd developed after the tornado. She quickly dropped them to her sides, "I'm fine," she said, and even she could hear the artificial cheer in her voice.

Dorian gazed into her eyes like he was trying to see into her soul. Maybe he was. "Em, is something wrong? Did I—"

"No," she cut him off. "It's not you. The cardinal in the window"—she pointed to the beautiful ornament—"made me think of my grandmother, that's all. She loves cardinals."

"Why cardinals? Does she like red?"

"No, she told me when you see a cardinal it means that someone you love who has passed is visiting. That they usually show up when you most need them or miss them to let you know they will always be with you."

Dorian was quiet for a moment. "That's beautiful," he murmured. "I didn't know that."

"Yeah, after my parents were killed, my grandmother started collecting them. My mom was her only child."

"You're close, you and your grandmother?"

"Very. She took me in after the—you know. She's the only family I have left." Emmie paused for a moment, then continued, "She's been sick. That's why I took this job. To help pay for her medical care." She took a last look at the cardinal ornament, let out a shaky breath, and started walking again. She didn't need to burden him with her troubles. He was going to have enough of his own to worry about when they got back to the hotel. She forced a bright smile. "So, what's on your agenda for this evening?"

Dorian wrinkled his forehead and Emmie was unable to read the expression on his face. He finally shrugged his shoulders. "I guess I hadn't thought much about it. What do you usually do in the evenings?"

"I like to watch movies and eat ice cream."

"Ice cream?"

"Yes, I *love* ice cream. Too much probably," she laughed.

"I can't remember the last time I had ice cream."

"Really?" Emmie asked incredulously. "Ice cream is probably my favorite thing to eat, especially when things are going wrong. Don't you have a favorite food?"

"Yes," Dorian grinned. "Grilled Mac Daddy-O sandwiches."

Emmie laughed. They had reached the hotel and Dorian stopped to let Gatsby do his business before they went inside. She wasn't looking forward to the reception she knew would be waiting for them when they returned. It was silly really. They were both adults. But she knew that with his title, Dorian had different responsibilities than most people.

A chill went down her back as Dorian pulled the door open, and they stepped into the lobby. Emmie was blinded by flashes of light. Questions came at her from every direction. Her chest tightened, and she was having a hard time catching her breath when she felt hands grip her arms. It was Chet. He pulled her toward the private elevator on their right. She turned and saw Trevor and Brody with Dorian and Gatsby. Relief washed over her until she saw who was waiting in the elevator.

CHAPTER 13

"Mother," Dorian's stomach tightened. *What was she doing here?* A flush of heat surged up his neck and across his face. *Was she checking up on him?* He stepped into the elevator. He'd scooped up Gatsby as soon as he saw the paparazzi and the dog trembled in his arms. He gently stroked Gatsby's fur, trying to comfort the frightened dog. He should have known he'd be unable to avoid them the entire day. He slid a glance to Emmie, who was standing next to Chet, arms crossed over her chest. Her face was pale and pinched. *How had he allowed this to happen?*

Queen Sophia smiled and waved at the reporters before the elevator doors closed. The tension in the air was palpable. He watched his mother look him up and down and registered disdain in her eyes.

"Mother, what are you doing here?" Dorian demanded after the elevator doors closed.

Sophia pursed her lips. "We shall discuss this in private."

They rode to their floor in an uncomfortable silence. The elevator doors opened. Dorian placed Gatsby on the floor once they entered the suite. Gatsby immediately ran into Dorian's room, head down and tail tucked. He clearly wanted no part of the discussion that was about to take place. Neither did Dorian. He wanted to watch movies and eat ice cream with Emmie, not get lectured by his mother.

Sophia dismissed the bodyguards to the other side of the suite and walked slowly and deliberately into the living room. She confronted Dorian and Emmie with narrowed eyes.

Dorian glanced at Emmie, and gave her what he hoped was an encouraging smile, and stood next to her into the living room.

"What on earth is going on here, Dorian? And *what* are you wearing?" Sophia snapped.

Dorian glanced down at his recycled clothing and clenched his jaw. He'd been raised not to challenge his mother, but he was tired of his life being dictated by her. He doubted she'd understand how liberating this afternoon had been.

"Nothing is *going on*, Mother. What are you doing here?"

Sophia pursed her lips and stared daggers at him. "Since you had a free evening in your schedule, I made arrangements for us to attend a charity event together. If you had been here"—the queen lifted an eyebrow, her gaze flitting over Emmie before settling on Dorian—"you would have been notified. Now, it appears I must also do damage control before

Avington is involved in yet another scandal because of you."

The blood rushed to Dorian's face. "Now wait just a minute," he countered. "There was no scandal. Candace fabricated that entire story. You *know* what she said wasn't true." *She did, didn't she?*

He had only dated Candace for a few months before he realized she was far more interested in what his title could do for her than she was in him. Once he'd caught on and called it off, she'd gone straight to the media implying he had been a liar and a cheat. Then, to top it all off, she'd accused him of using his title and influence to bribe an umpire in a cricket tournament. Because it was the royal family's policy not to comment on tabloid stories, Dorian hadn't had an opportunity to air his side, and it had not done well for his approval rating in Avington.

Sophia snorted. "Candace used you to get her name on every newsstand in this country. To further her career because of you." She shot a fiery gaze at

Emmie and pointed a finger at her. "Just like Miss Walker is trying to do. She's nothing more than another American gold-digger."

Dorian opened his mouth to respond, but Emmie stepped forward before he could get a word out.

"Excuse me?" She gripped one hand on her hip and stared at his mother, her face full of anger. "I don't know what kind of *scandal* you're talking about, but I resent being called a gold-digger."

Dorian was dumbfounded. In all his life, he'd never heard anyone talk to his mother this way and he knew Sophia was probably losing her mind over what she would consider to be Emmie's insolence.

Sophia glared at Emmie and sniffed. "You've managed to wheedle your way into the media with my son, even though you were expressly forbidden from doing so. You should be able to make a tidy profit selling stories about our family."

"Why would I..." Emmie stumbled over her words. "Why would I do that? Just because that *actress* ran her mouth off, it doesn't mean *every* American woman is devoid of values. Dorian is the kindest, most generous man I've ever met. A trait he clearly didn't inherit from you." Her face was flaming hot and tears blurred her vision.

Sophia gasped. "Miss Walker!"

Dorian stepped between them and raised his hands, directing his attention toward his mother. "Let's not get carried away," he said in what he hoped was a soothing voice. This was getting out of control. Fast.

"I will not be spoken to like that." Sophia splayed a perfectly manicured hand across her chest, her face ashen. "I knew I shouldn't have allowed Mr. Harrison to hire a woman, let alone an American." Sophia gave Emmie a disapproving scowl before she turned to Dorian with fury in her eyes. "But then I saw her and figured she wasn't your type. I never considered you'd make a fool out of yourself over this—this opportunist. Look at you," she snapped with a dismissive wave of her hand. "You look like a pauper!"

"Mother," Dorian warned.

"According to our background search, she barely has a penny to her name. She doesn't even have a place of her own to live. She's leeching off her elderly grandmother. Look at what she's wearing! She's the worst kind of citizen, Dorian. A poor American who is going to ruin you."

"That's enough!" Dorian bellowed. Sophia shrank back, holding on to the fireplace mantel with one hand as if to steady herself. He tried to reassure Emmie with a smile, but her face was flushed and her mouth agape. "I happen to *like* what she's wearing and—"

Emmie rested her hand on his upper arm and gave him a slight shove so she could step around him, her eyes blazing. "I may not be rich," she told Sophia in a low, controlled voice, "or wear designer clothing, and I may not live in a huge house or a castle, but I would *never* treat my family the way you are treating your son."

She glanced between Dorian and his mother, the tears welling in her eyes a moment ago now spilling over her lashes and running down her cheeks. "Do you know how lucky you are to have each other? What a gift that is?" Emmie took a deep breath, her gaze meeting his. "And I would *never* betray you, I hope you know that," she said softly. "But I don't need this either. I'm sorry Dorian, I quit." She turned on her heel and walked away.

"Emmie, wait!" Dorian called, but Emmie put her hand up to stop him without looking back. He watched her walk stiffly to her room and shut the door behind her. Dorian admired her for being strong enough to stand up for herself, but she shouldn't have had to do that. Anger flowed through him as he turned to his mother.

"That was completely unnecessary," he said in a low voice. "You went too far, Mother. You don't know her. She isn't like that."

"You thought Candace was captivating right away too."

"Emmie is *nothing* like Candace."

"You don't *know* her, Dorian."

"I do," he argued. "You're making more out of it than you need to. We aren't involved. She *works* for me." The words sounded lame to his ears, even as they came out of his mouth. While Emmie may work for him, she was all he could think about.

Sophia walked to the couch and sat, patting the space beside her. Dorian took a steeling breath and sat next to her.

"I've seen how you look at her, Dorian. It's my job to protect our family."

"By insulting her?"

"How can you possibly think you know her after such a short period of time?"

Even though he'd only known her for a couple of weeks, Dorian felt he'd known Emmie far longer. He was more comfortable being himself around Emmie than he was with anyone else. He took a deep breath. "I don't know. I just do."

"She's a bad influence, Dorian. You *ran away* from your bodyguards."

Dorian sighed. "I didn't run away from them. I just needed some breathing space. Emmie had nothing to do with that. That was *my* idea."

Sophia studied him with a mixture of skepticism and concern. "You put your life in danger."

"I was a combat pilot in Afghanistan," he pointed out. "My life was in far more danger there than it was on Beale Street with Emmie."

Sophia pursed her lips. "You have bodyguards for a reason," she insisted.

"I know. But don't you ever get tired of constantly being watched? No matter where you go?"

Sophia stared thoughtfully for a long moment, her gaze focused on something only she could see as the expression on her face softened. She absently twisted the emerald coronation ring on the ring finger of her right hand. Her gaze, now cold and closed off, returned to his. Her chin lifted, "We have a responsibility to our people. To our country. Part of that responsibility is to remain safe to carry out our duties."

Dorian fought the urge to groan. On one hand, he could see her point. But on the other, she had to wish she could run a simple errand without a motorcade and armed escorts, didn't she? He pinched the bridge of his nose. She would never understand him. Even when he was a young child, she hadn't understood him. Sophia and Philip were cut from the same cloth, which was fitting since Philip was heir to the throne. Dorian had always been more like his father, Prince Andrew.

Andrew had exhibited a zest for life and sense of adventure that ultimately ended up being his undoing. Dorian had taken after him in that way, always choosing his own path instead of the one carefully laid out for him. Sophia loved opera, where Andrew had preferred the Beatles. Andrew had loved racing cars. Sophia hated it. When Andrew was killed in an auto race when Dorian was ten years old, Sophia had banned the sport of auto racing from Avington. Sophia and Andrew were so different, Dorian often wondered how they had ever married in the first place.

"I understand we have responsibilities," he said. "Part of my trip here has been to learn and make arrangements so I can carry out my duties as a representative of Avington when I return. Yes, I ditched my bodyguards, but it's not a big deal. I'm fine."

"You could have been kidnapped or killed," the queen cried, her voice rising as she spoke. "It certainly is a big deal."

"But I wasn't. I highly doubt an assassin was waiting on Beale Street in the hopes that I would just happen to be there without security."

She reached out and touched the sleeve of his T-shirt. "And wearing this? You look like a derelict."

He looked down at his jeans and T-shirt, then back to her. "We bought them. Emmie thought if I stayed in the suit, I would attract more attention. They're actually very comfortable."

"What kind of store sells...rags?"

Dorian had to fight to suppress a chuckle as he answered, "A recycled clothing store."

Sophia's mouth opened, forming a perfect O, the color draining from her face. She brought a hand to her throat. "*Used* clothing? You are wearing *used* clothing?"

"Emmie thought I would blend in better wearing this and she was right," Dorian smirked. "No one recognized me all afternoon."

Sophia's eyes narrowed and her lip curled up in a sneer. "Miss Walker again. I should have known she was behind this. She is trying to make you look like a fool! How am I going to explain this to the Council?"

Dorian let out a sardonic laugh. "What does the Council care? I'll never be on the throne. And what's there to explain? These are *clothes,* Mother. I wasn't photographed nude in a hotel room like a member of a different royal family."

"That is not our business," Sophia shot back. "You are here as an ambassador of Avington. How does it look to the world if you are...cavorting with the staff? Make that former staff."

Her words reminded Dorian that Emmie had quit. He couldn't let that happen. He wasn't ready to let her go yet. "She's the best dog handler I've ever seen, and I will not have you bully her into quitting."

"She already has."

"Not if I have anything to do with it."

Sophia's mouth pressed into a thin line. "It will never work, Dorian. She's a citizen. An *American* citizen."

"I don't care," Dorian rose to his feet and shouted. "I don't care! I don't care that she's American. I don't care that she's not aristocracy." He spun around and strode toward the door. He paused and looked over his shoulder to meet his mother's icy gaze. "It's not your choice, Mother."

Sophia patted her hair, throwing a derisive look at him. "We'll see about that," she muttered. "Go make yourself presentable. The car is waiting."

CHAPTER 14

Emmie flopped on the bed and pulled the pillow over her face. How could she have let things get so out of control between her and Dorian? Why couldn't she just stick to the rules? No consorting. It wasn't rocket science. And why had she quit? How was she going to pay for her grandmother's medical care now? She'd been so foolish.

It was times like this that Emmie wished she had a close friend. When she'd gone to live with her grandmother after her mom and dad had been killed, she'd struggled with making friends. She was self-conscious of her scars and her left leg had been badly damaged, requiring Emmie to endure several painful surgeries and months on crutches, and then in a brace. Sensing her granddaughter's plight, her grandmother involved Emmie in the local 4-H dog program. 4-H was a free youth program offered through the county. It was there she discovered her passion for dogs, and where she had met Ashley.

Ashley White and Emmie had become fast friends and were inseparable through high school. Ashley's family couldn't afford to send her to college, so Ashley decided to join the military after they graduated. She and Emmie planned to open a dog training facility together when she was done with her enlistment. Emmie would train the dogs and Ashley would run the office. They'd both get married and live next door to each other so their kids could be best friends too. Then Ashley was killed in the war and Emmie felt like she'd lost a sister. She closed herself off from everyone after that, focusing instead on the dogs she worked with.

Until Dorian. Emmie knew she couldn't have him. *Why had she let him in?* Maybe it was because of the way he looked at her; like no one else ever had. Maybe it was because she felt she could talk to him about anything. Maybe it was because she could get lost in his eyes forever and never want to find her way out.

Snap out of it! She couldn't waste her time daydreaming about something that could never happen. What she needed to be thinking about was what she was going to do when she got back to Minnesota. She needed a job, and fast. Her grandmother was relying on her.

Nana. Emmie missed her so badly it hurt. The thought of losing her was almost more than she could bear. A tightness took hold of her throat. Her chest felt like it had been wrapped in a band that was slowly constricting, and her breaths came faster as she struggled to fill her lungs with oxygen. She sat up and tried to slow her breathing. The room tilted, and she closed her eyes. She knew she needed to take slow, deep breaths, and slow her racing heart. If she could just focus.

A scratching sound came from outside the door. *Gatsby.* Emmie opened her eyes and made her way to the door, opening it just enough to let the dog slip in. She picked him up and buried her face in his soft fur, feeling the sense of panic ease with each stroke of her hand down his back.

"Gatsby, I don't know what you're doing here, but thank you." She plopped down on the bed next to him and let herself fall backwards. Gatsby settled in beside her and rested his head on her shoulder, his deep brown eyes staring into hers.

"Oh, if I could only read your mind, Duke." Emmie patted the dog on top of his head and absently stroked the fur on his back. "I'm going to miss you. You and your dad." A tear slid down the side of her face, into her hair. Her grandmother had always told her that when God closed one door, he opened another. Right now, Emmie felt she'd spent a lifetime looking at closed doors.

God, if you have a door ready for me, I really wish you'd show me where it is.

She sat back up and Gatsby rolled onto his back, a derpy expression on his face. She gazed at the corgi, wishing he could talk so she could ask him what to do. He'd side with Dorian, of course, but still...

Emmie fished her phone out of her purse. She knew her grandmother would be disappointed in her for quitting the way she did, but she needed to talk to someone. She dialed the number for her grandmother's room at the hospital. It rang several times before Agnes's voice answered.

"Hello?"

"Hi Agnes, it's Emmie. How's Na--"

"Emmeline, honey. How wonderful to hear from you! Blanche told me you've been seeing a prince, of all things!"

Not her too. "No, we're not--"

"I told my granddaughter to set her sights high too, but did she listen to me? *No*, she went and ran off with a long-haired rock and roll player. And honey, I do mean player. Back in my day, we called girls that did that groupies," Agnes tsked. "But you, you got yourself a *real live prince*."

"Agnes, it's not like that." Emmie was beginning to feel like a broken record. "I work--worked for him. That's all. Is—"

"Nonsense, Blanche showed me a picture of you with that prince on one of them smart phones. I don't know why they think they're so smart, must be that you need to be smart to use them," she laughed. "Anyways, my eyesight isn't what it used to be, but honey, I can see when two people are head over heels for each other." She paused for just a second. "Wait, did you just say 'worked'?"

"Yes, I--we--I—there was an incident today and—and I told him I quit." Emmie was glad Agnes couldn't see the shame she knew was on her face, yet she felt relief in being able to tell someone what she'd done, even if it was her grandmother's best friend. She heard a sharp intake of breath on the other end of the phone.

"Oh Emmeline, you mustn't quit," Agnes blurted out. "Your grandmother is so proud of you, and she's told me how important this job is for you. She said your future is in this job—or maybe it was that your future was with that good-looking prince."

Emmie grimaced, closed her eyes, and let out a frustrated breath. "Agnes, where is Nana?"

"Oh right. She's asleep dear. They gave her some stronger pain medicine and it makes her sleepy."

Emmie furrowed her brow. "Stronger pain medicine? Agnes, is there a nurse I can talk to?"

Emmie spent the next ten minutes on the phone talking to her grandmother's nurse. The cancer was far more advanced than Emmie had been told. The prognosis was not good and because Nana had waited so long to come in, and the cancer was so aggressive, treatment options were slim. Even if she received treatment, which she had refused, she'd be buying a couple of months at the most.

They would keep her in the hospital until she was more stable. When Emmie returned, they would talk about the possibility of letting her grandmother move back home and getting her set up with a home health nurse to come and check on her a couple times a week. When Emmie asked how long she had, the nurse paused and said it was hard to tell. With lung cancer at this late stage, she could last a few months, or she could go very quickly. Emmie thanked her and hung up the phone. Her ears began to ring and the edges of her vision blurred. Her grandmother, the only family she had left in the world, was dying.

There was a soft knock on the door and Emmie jumped, her heart racing from the unexpected sound. Gatsby struggled into a sitting position, his large ears pointed skyward, his head tilted slightly to the side. Emmie didn't want to see anyone. She just wanted...she didn't know. To be alone? The knock sounded again. Maybe it was Dorian. She closed her eyes as she struggled to regain some semblance of composure. What if it was his mother? She groaned and slid off the bed, slowly making her way to the door. She held her hand on the lock for a moment before she finally turned it, the click of the tumblers resonating in her ears. She wasn't ready to face the proverbial music, so rather than open the door, she just walked back to the bed, sat, and waited. Her hand resting on Gatsby's back.

The door opened slightly and Emmie was surprised to see Montgomery on the other side of it. The older man held the door open just enough to peek into the room.

"Miss Walker, would you mind coming out here so we can talk?" He had the same polite tone to his voice as always, but his eyes were warm and his voice soft.

Emmie rose and placed Gatsby on the floor. Letting out a long breath, she gave Montgomery a weak smile. *Might as well get it over with.*

"Sure," she said and followed him out to the kitchen.

Montgomery motioned for Emmie to take a seat on one of the stools at the counter. She climbed onto the chair, wrapped her feet around its tall legs and rubbed at an invisible smudge on the counter with her finger.

He opened the freezer and took out at least a dozen pints of ice cream, in assorted flavors. "I'm guessing you could use one of these about now."

Emmie jaw unhinged as she looked from the ice cream back to Montgomery. "How did you—?"

"His Highness said that ice cream was your favorite comfort food and if anyone needed comfort food right now, he guessed it would be you. He sent Chet out for some before he left. Not knowing what flavor you liked, he told Chet to get one of everything."

Emmie's eyes filled with tears, much to her embarrassment, and she covered her face with her hands. Between the confusing feelings she had for Dorian, the encounter with his mother, and the phone conversation about her grandmother, she'd had about all she could handle for one day. Having Dorian remember that she loved ice cream when she was stressed just pushed her emotions over the edge.

"Miss Walker, are you all right?" Montgomery asked, confusion in his voice.

Emmie sniffed and wiped her eyes with her hands. "Yes, I'm sorry. It's been a long day."

"Then please, help yourself." He gestured to the cartons of ice cream.

Emmie looked at the variety of flavors and selected salted caramel fudge swirl. Montgomery handed her a spoon, selected a pint for himself, and returned the remaining ice cream to the freezer. Emmie pulled the lid off her container and slid a spoonful of the frozen treat into her mouth. It was the perfect combination of rich chocolate and decadent caramel with a hint of salt to balance out the sweet, set in a creamy vanilla-bean-flavored base. This was exactly what she needed.

Montgomery took a spoon of his ice cream. Emmie noticed he'd chosen Maple Nut, which was also her grandmother's favorite. "This is good," he said. "I can't remember the last time I had ice cream."

"Life is better with ice cream," Emmie replied and looked around, noticing for the first time that she and Montgomery were alone. "Where did everyone go?"

"A charity event at The Cadre."

Emmie nodded and steeled herself. "I know we aren't here to eat ice cream and do each-other's hair, Montgomery. What's up?"

Montgomery ran a hand across his bald head and chuckled. "You do have a way with words, Miss Walker." He leaned against the counter opposite where Emmie sat. "His Highness told me you'd quit."

Emmie nodded her head, the corners of her mouth turned down. "I did," she said softly.

"I'd like you to reconsider."

Emmie's head snapped up and her mouth opened, her soul filled with confusion. "But I can't, I–I..." What could she say in her defense? She'd told off *the queen*. She was lucky it was modern times because she was sure she'd have been beheaded for doing something so brazen—make that *foolish*—back in...back in the times when they did that sort of thing.

"Yes, I heard you and Her Majesty had words."

Did they all know? Emmie's cheeks flamed and she covered her mouth with her hands, embarrassed by her actions. "I may have said a few things I shouldn't have," she murmured through her fingers, then lowered her hands to the counter and slumped in her chair.

"On the contrary, Miss Walker."

Wait, what? Emmie straightened and tipped her head to the side.

"You were defending your reputation. There is no shame in that," Montgomery said. "The manner of delivery, however, could use some work." A hint of a smile crossed his lips.

"There's no way Dorian will want me to stay after how I spoke to his mother—I mean the queen." She face-palmed herself. "The *queen*. She thinks I'm a gold-digger."

Montgomery's expression softened. "Her Majesty has a strong drive to protect her children and her experience with American women, particularly those connected with His Highness, has been less than positive in that regard."

Emmie considered that for a moment. "I can see where people like Candace Easton might give that impression, but not all Americans are like that."

"She can be a bit hasty in her judgements," Montgomery conceded. "But she's also in a position where a lapse in judgement can have detrimental consequences. She tends to be overly cautious, especially with the prince."

Emmie took another spoonful of ice cream and leaned forward on her elbows, resting her head in her hands. "I've made a real mess of things, haven't I?"

Montgomery shook his head. "Quite the opposite actually."

"What?"

"The changes you've made with Gatsby in such a short period of time are remarkable."

"I don't understand. Changes? I've worked on basic training with him, taught him a few tricks, but no big changes."

Montgomery chuckled. "He was quite a handful prior to your arrival. So much so that Howard played up his age issues to avoid having to travel with the dog."

"Oh, I had no idea. Howard's methods are a bit...outdated, but Gatsby is a smart dog. He's easy to train."

"For you." Montgomery paused and took another bite of his ice cream. He studied Emmie for a minute, like he was contemplating what he was going to say next. "And I've seen changes in His Highness too."

Emmie watched him intently but stayed silent. She had no idea where this was heading.

"I've known Dorian all his life," Montgomery continued, the use of the prince's given name not lost on Emmie. "He's been more confident, less uptight and more...himself than I've seen him in years. And I thought, what's different? It occurred to me today, when I heard he'd taken you and dodged his security team for the afternoon. It's you."

Emmie grimaced, "It wasn't my idea to do that."

"Which is exactly my point." Montgomery slapped his hand on the counter, a huge grin on his face.

"I don't understand."

"He's himself when he's with you. He isn't *the Prince of Avington*," Montgomery said, making air quotes with his fingers. "He's just Dorian. It's good to see that."

"His title doesn't define who he is."

"Oh, Miss Walker, but it does. Look at Her Majesty and Prince Philip. Their title *is* who they are. Prince Dorian is in a position to be able to have a blend of the two. You have helped him see that. Please reconsider your resignation."

"The queen said my presence was causing a scandal. I really don't think—"

"Miss Walker, I have worked for this family for more than thirty-five years. If I wrote a book about all the real scandals I've seen over the years, I'd be a very rich man. *This* "—he waved his hand in the air— "is not a scandal."

"But—"

"They need you, Emmie."

They need you. The words echoed in her head. Her grandmother needed her. She didn't know what the right answer was anymore. "I don't know, Montgomery. It's not that simple. I'll have to think about it."

CHAPTER 15

Dorian walked toward the kitchen, pausing for a moment at Emmie's door. It was closed and he didn't hear any sounds coming from inside. Resisting the urge to knock, he continued past the counter where Montgomery perched on one of the stools, drinking coffee and reading the newspaper.

"Good morning, Your Highness," Montgomery greeted him.

"Montgomery." Dorian nodded a greeting in return. "Is she still here?"

"If you are referring to Miss Walker, she is."

Dorian let out a deep breath as relief flooded through him. Smiling to himself, he reached for a coffee mug and poured himself a cup. "That's great news."

Montgomery studied him for a moment. "Indeed it is, Your Highness. And the charity event last night went well?"

Dorian sat on the stool next to Montgomery. "It was fine. The typical black-tie affair. Mother returned to Avington immediately following the event." The ride to the event had been very uncomfortable, but the rest of the evening was business as usual. Sophia traveled with a much larger entourage than Dorian, and she also used the private jet they owned. He knew she'd rest on the flight home and her staff would have her looking perfectly coiffed when she debarked from the plane upon her arrival in Avington.

"The tour is going quite well, Your Highness, all things considered," Montgomery observed. "The press has been very positive about your visits. It seems that bringing Gatsby to the Veterans Hospital and the Children's Hospital was a smart move."

"Yes, he was well received. The children in particular loved him. To be honest, I wasn't entirely sure it was a good idea," Dorian confided. "You know how he can be rather…"

"Difficult?"

Dorian shot a glance at Montgomery. "Stubborn. He responds so well to Emmie. She's made remarkable changes in his behavior. We are bringing him to Troop Packs today. The kids will love playing with him."

"Yes, Gatsby has made much progress in a very short period of time." Montgomery paused. Dorian could read the indecision in his eyes. "I've noticed changes in you too," his private secretary finally continued.

Dorian tensed. "What do you mean?"

"I've known you a long time, Your Highness. If I may, you seem much more relaxed on this trip than you have been for some time. And there was your adventure yesterday. You seem...happy. And I'm wondering if Miss Walker isn't the cause of the difference in you as well."

Dorian took a moment to consider what Montgomery said. He knew Emmie made him feel it was okay to be himself, not the romanticized image that most other people had because of his title. She made him feel...whole.

His grandmother had always told him that each person was created as a whole that was then split in two—a man and a woman. They were then destined to roam the earth trying to find their other half. Some never do, but others are more fortunate and when they find their other half, it's like magic. He'd always dismissed that story as just that, a story, but now he was beginning to wonder if there wasn't something to it.

Is Emmie my magic?

The door to Emmie's room opened and she emerged. She was wearing black pants and a mint-colored shirt with a black floral duster over the top. Her long hair was loose and flowed down her back. How could she look so good no matter what she was wearing? Emmie's gaze briefly met his as she walked into the kitchen and poured herself a cup of coffee. She hesitated, pushing a strand of hair behind her ear and her gaze flitted between him and Montgomery, uncertainty playing across her features.

"Good morning, Emmie," he smiled. "Will you join me with your coffee?"

"Miss Walker," Montgomery nodded in greeting, then turned to Dorian. "I'll be in the other room if you need me, Your Highness."

Dorian waited while Montgomery ambled out of the room, Emmie taking his place on the stool next to him. Dorian swiveled so he was facing her. "I'm so glad you've decided to stay."

Her chin quivered and Dorian noticed dark circles under her eyes. He felt at once both an overwhelming need to comfort her and a pang of fear that she'd changed her mind and was leaving.

She took a deep breath and slowly let it out. "Dorian, I'm so sorry for yesterday. I had no business sassing Queen Sophia that way—"

"Em—"

Emmie held up her hand to stop him, "I'm not done." She gave him a weak smile. "Regardless of her title, she's your mother too, and it was really disrespectful of me. I don't know that I'll have a chance to see her before I leave to properly apologize, but I promise it will never happen again."

Dorian ached to hold her in his arms but reached for her hands instead. They were small compared to his, and soft, and very cold. He squeezed them gently and looked into her beautiful honey colored eyes. "Em, it's all right. It was an unfortunate situation that was taken entirely too far."

"But she is the *Queen of Avington*. I may be American, but even I know you aren't supposed to sass a queen, no matter what she's said..." She chewed her lip. "It won't happen again."

"I'm sorry she called you a gold-digger. I would say it's a draw."

"Thanks, Dorian." She took a trembling breath, her gaze locked into his.

Dorian's gaze dropped to her lips before returning to her eyes. Emmie pulled her hands away, her face a mask of worry.

"Thank you too for letting me stay on. I can be impulsive sometimes and shouldn't have quit. I need this job." She blinked and looked away, gripping her coffee mug and staring into the dark liquid within. "I'll finish out the remainder of my contract."

Dorian's stomach rolled. Emmie would be gone at the end of the week. His heart hurt just thinking about it. He had only a few days to convince her to stay. Maybe he could offer her a permanent job at the castle. No, that would create a scandal for sure. He wasn't sure what he was going to do. He only knew that he didn't want his time with her to end this soon. She was still staring into her mug, as though she didn't know what to say. Her hair had fallen forward but Dorian could see the sadness in her face. He placed his hand on her arm. "Emmie, are you okay?"

She stifled a yawn, then turned to look at him, offering a small smile. "Yes. I didn't sleep well and just need more coffee. The caffeine hasn't kicked in yet."

He withdrew his hand and rose, his lips turning upward in a grin. "I can help you with that." He brought the coffee pot over to her and refilled both their mugs.

Leaning toward him, she nudged him with her elbow before she straightened back up. "Thanks for the ice cream, by the way. That was really sweet."

Dorian grinned. "Ice cream is *supposed* to be sweet."

"You know what I mean."

"There's plenty left, maybe we can have some later?"

Emmie studied him for a moment as if trying to determine if he really meant it, then smiled back. "Yes, that would be great."

The sound of little feet padding across the carpet then the tile interrupted their conversation and provided a welcome relief for the awkwardness that had formed between them. Gatsby put his front feet on Dorian's leg. He held a stuffed monkey toy in his mouth and moved his jaw, repeatedly making the monkey squeak. Dorian laughed.

"Good morning to you too, Duke." He'd taken to calling the dog by the nickname Emmie had given him. Dorian wrestled the toy from Gatsby's mouth and gave it a toss. The dog ran after it with glee, returning a few seconds later to drop it at Dorian's feet, his eyes glimmering with pride. Dorian scooped up the dog and held him in his lap. Emmie reached over and ruffled the fur on Gatsby's head, who reveled in the attention.

"How did you come up with the name 'Gatsby'?" Emmie asked.

"He was a gift from my grandmother shortly before she passed, and she named him."

"What a great gift. That must make him extra special. Was she a fan of F. Scott Fitzgerald then?"

Dorian laughed. "No, Leonardo DiCaprio. She loved him in the movie Gatsby. She thought he looked so debonair."

"She sounds like a unique lady."

"She was the best. I believe I still have a little bit of her with me in Gatsby."

"You're lucky to have him."

They spent the day at Troop Packs working with family and friends of deployed service members to create care packages for them. As Dorian expected, the children went crazy for Gatsby, and they had a blast playing while Emmie watched over them. She appeared to be having as much fun as they did, and Dorian enjoyed watching her while she answered what seemed to be at least a hundred questions from the children's inquisitive minds. *She'd make a great mother,* he thought and then chastised himself for thinking it. She was leaving at the end of the week. He returned his focus to the care packages.

Dorian listened to stories of families who were waiting for loved ones to return and their joys and hardships while dealing with a deployed family member. While he was in Afghanistan, he'd observed members of his troop receiving care packages like these and he knew how much they meant to weary, homesick soldiers. He was proud to help put the packs together. Not just showing up for a photo op, but to get involved and make a difference.

Each package, in addition to the necessities such as socks, sunscreen and soap, contained a hand-written note to the soldier who would receive it thanking them for their service and sacrifice, as well as sending an inspirational message of encouragement. Dorian even wrote several notes himself. He posed for photos and selfies with anyone that wanted them and gave out many hugs before they left to return to the hotel.

They climbed into the waiting limo. Emmie secured a very sleepy Gatsby into his seat and sat next to Kate. Dorian thought she looked tired and maybe a little preoccupied. He left her to her thoughts and gazed out his window, watching the people walking along Beale Street. He chuckled to himself when they passed *Thrifty Blues*. They were driving past the park when he recognized a brightly colored food truck. He pressed the button to lower the privacy partition window. "Please stop here, now," he told the driver, a sense of urgency in his voice.

"Your Highness, what are you doing?" Brody asked, concerned, as the limo pulled to the side of the street.

"I'm going to get us an order of sandwiches," Dorian said. "You've *got* to try these!" He caught Emmie's eye, and gave her a quick wink before reaching for the door handle.

"Your Highness, I must insist that you allow Brody or Trevor to procure your sandwich," Kate said, her brows furrowed, and her chin lifted. "We cannot risk having the paparazzi catching you off-guard again."

Dorian was about to protest but thought about the fallout from his mother if that were to happen.

He'd managed to smooth things over with her by the end of the evening the night before and wasn't about to risk incurring her wrath again. He pulled his wallet from the pocket of his chinos, extracted several bills and handed them to Brody.

"Go to the *Say Cheese* truck," Dorian pointed to the bright yellow food truck. Brody peered out the window and back to him, his head flinching backward. "Order ten of the Mac Daddy-O sandwiches," Dorian continued.

Brody looked confused. "Ten, Your Highness?"

"Yes, add fries too."

Brody did as he was told and once they got back to the hotel, Dorian distributed the meal. Everyone loved the Mac Daddy-O's, including Kate. After they'd finished eating, Kate and Montgomery left to get the jet ready for their flight to Los Angeles in the morning, and the bodyguards rented a pay-per-view movie on the other side of the suite.

Dorian stood and stretched. It had been a long afternoon and he was looking forward to the light schedule tomorrow. Emmie had been uncharacteristically quiet since they left Troop Packs and he wasn't sure if something was wrong or if she was just tired. She'd gotten up right after she finished her sandwich and settled on the sofa in the living room with Gatsby.

Dorian grabbed two pints of ice cream from the freezer, along with two spoons and placed them on the coffee table. Emmie lifted her head and gave him a grateful smile. His heart skipped a beat inside his chest; she was so beautiful, even when she was tired.

"Look what I found in my shopping bag." Dorian pulled the stuffed bear she'd been given at the Children's Hospital from under his arm and handed it to her.

"Charlie!" she exclaimed. "Thank you, Dorian. I thought I'd lost him."

She took it from him and hugged it close, and he wondered what her arms would feel like around him. A strange feeling welled up inside him. He wasn't sure what it meant but he knew he didn't want this week to end.

"He was missing you." Dorian settled on the sofa next to her. Gatsby stretched out on her other side, fast asleep. He handed Emmie one of the pints of ice cream and a spoon, then pried the lid off his. "This looks really good."

They talked for several minutes about their experience at Troop Packs while enjoying their ice cream before deciding to watch a movie.

"I can't believe you haven't seen *Pretty Woman*," Emmie chuckled. "Don't you have theaters in Avington?"

"What?" Dorian threw his hands up in mock defense, nearly dropping his ice cream in the process. "Of course, we have theaters. We usually get European releases though, not American and…well,

I guess I don't watch very many." He couldn't remember the last time he'd seen a film, actually.

"Hmm, well this is a classic. You'll love it." Emmie searched through the movie app until she found it and pressed play, then leaned back into the sofa, her shoulder resting against his. He fought the urge to wrap his arm around her. Instead, he leaned over her and stuck his spoon in her pint.

"Hey, ice cream thief!" she cried through a giggle.

"I just want to try yours. What flavor is it? It's for research purposes," he smirked, trying to sound very official.

"Research, huh? Well, I can't argue with that I guess," she held the pint closer, so he was able to spoon some out. "It's vanilla Swiss almond."

He stuck the spoon in his mouth and groaned, it was so good. He'd have to make sure the kitchen back home was sufficiently stocked with a variety of flavors when he returned.

"What do you have? Chocolate?" she asked, trying to peer into his container.

"Sort of, it's chocolate fudge brownie and I'll let you try it, but only in the name of research." He filled his spoon and held it up to her, their gazes locking as she took the ice cream in her mouth.

"It's really good," she murmured and ran her tongue across her lip.

Dorian's gaze traveled to her mouth, and he wondered if her lips tasted as sweet as his ice cream. He had to find out. He leaned in, every nerve in his body humming in anticipation.

The door to the suite burst open, and Montgomery and Kate entered, laughing. Dorian and Emmie flew apart, Emmie's face flushed a bright red. She rose and stretched, and Dorian cursed their timing.

"You know, I didn't sleep well last night and I'm really tired. I think I'm going to turn in," Emmie announced, hugging Charlie bear to her chest. Her gaze lingered on Dorian for a moment before she turned and retreated to her room.

"I hope we didn't interrupt anything," Montgomery gave Dorian a knowing glance. Kate pursed her lips and disappeared into the other side of the suite.

Dorian flopped back on the sofa and ran his hands through his hair. Montgomery took a seat on one of the chairs next to the sofa. "You really care about her, don't you?"

Dorian released a heavy sigh. "I don't know. I mean, yes. I know...it's just all wrong," he said, leaning forward and resting his elbows on his knees.

"How so?"

"Well, for starters, she *works* for me. I know I shouldn't cross that line. Plus, she's an American on top of it. It's totally illogical for me to think of her like that."

Montgomery sat quietly for a moment, then stood up and walked to the couch next to where

Dorian sat. He placed a hand on Dorian's shoulder and squeezed it in a gentle, fatherly fashion. "It's been my experience that love has very little to do with logic." He bid Dorian goodnight and left the room.

Love? It can't be love, can it? Dorian pondered that while he watched the rest of the movie. In some ways the story made him think of him and Emmie, well, except for the hooker part. An idea began to form in his mind. He went to his room to get his phone. He looked at the clock to figure the time difference and found the number he was looking for in his contacts list. It would be 7:00 a.m. at home. He pressed the call button and waited.

"Hello? Dorian, is everything ok?"

"Anna, yes, everything is fine. I didn't wake you and Philip, did I?"

"No, Archer's up already. What's wrong?"

"Anna, I need your help—"

CHAPTER 16

THE SLEEK WHITE PRIVATE jet cruised at 41,000 feet heading from Memphis to Los Angeles. Emmie had never flown in one and was awestruck at the extravagance. It looked more like the living area of a suite than the inside of a plane. She clipped Gatsby into his special seat and sat next to him on the long leather sofa. Dorian was on the flight deck with the pilot. He wore a headset and was deep in conversation, pointing at the various gauges and controls on the instrument panel.

Emmie's mind drifted to the night before. Would Dorian have really kissed her if Montgomery and

Kate hadn't shown up? Would she have let him? A surge of warmth spread through her as she wondered what his lips would taste like, what they would feel like pressed against hers.

She knew there wasn't a chance of things working out with him; she was too far removed from his lifestyle, his status. Why was he even showing an interest in her? She was nothing special. She didn't even look like the other women she'd seen on his arm in the magazines. Perhaps she was just a novelty for him. But it didn't feel like that. Being with him felt natural and comfortable...and...and right. Emmie could no longer deny the growing attraction she had for him. What to do about it was the issue. Deciding she needed a distraction, Emmie picked up a copy of *Good Housekeeping* magazine from the rack by her seat and spent the rest of the flight paging through it.

After a textbook landing, the group took a limo to the posh hotel in Beverly Hills they'd be staying at for the next two days. The driver opened the doors and Emmie was just about to unbuckle her belt when Dorian touched her hand, stopping her. She stared at him, not comprehending. He smiled and held up one finger.

"Montgomery, please take Gatsby to the room and see that he's fed and given fresh water," Dorian directed. Montgomery looked unfazed by his request and Emmie knew something was up, but what was it?

"Trevor, you'll stay with me and Emmie. The rest of you can get settled in the hotel. You can all have the afternoon off."

Kate gaped at him. She opened her mouth as if to say something, but then closed it, hesitating for an instant before getting out of the car. Then she ducked her head back in. "Thank you, Your Highness." She grinned and practically skipped into the hotel. Emmie swore the woman seemed almost giddy.

"I didn't know she could smile," Emmie said.

He chuckled. "She's really not that bad once you get to know her."

"How very diplomatic of you," she laughed.

The limo pulled away from the hotel, the driver clearly having been given a destination beforehand. Frowning slightly, Emmie asked. "Where are we going?"

Dorian beamed at her, looking like a kid in a candy store. "I'd like you to accompany me to the Animal Rescue Gala tomorrow."

"But I'm already going to be there. With Gatsby."

"Yes, and you will still be there with Gatsby. But I'd like you to be there with me as well."

What? He couldn't possibly be asking her on a date, could he?

"I don't understand. You mean like a...?" Her mind refused to let her mouth say the word.

Dorian nodded. "Date."

Heat flooded her cheeks. A date. With a prince, no - make that *the* prince. She had to be dreaming. She cut a quick glance at Trevor and the shocked expression on his face confirmed that she was indeed awake. Her mind was in a daze. She'd never been to a formal event before. Well, never as a guest anyway. That would mean she'd need—

"A dress!" she blurted out. "I can't go. I don't have a dress."

Dorian took her hands in his and looked at her intently, his expression soft, and his eyes bright. *Oh, but the man was gorgeous.*

"After you left for your room last night, I finished watching that movie. You're right, it *is* good. And it inspired me. I'm taking you shopping."

Emmie laughed, "Be serious, Dorian." A flicker of disappointment crossed his handsome features. He *was* serious. She squeezed his hands. "I'm sorry, I thought—I don't know what I thought, I guess—I just—why? Why me? You could take anyone."

Dorian leaned back and studied her for a moment. "Because I like you."

The limo stopped on Rodeo Drive in Beverly Hills and Trevor escorted them into a posh clothing boutique. They rode an elevator to the third floor where a tall, willowy woman led them into a lavish private sitting area with luxurious silk-lined walls. A plush white upholstered sofa sat in the center of the room, flanked on either side by matching chairs. Along the far wall, an open curtain revealed a large fitting room with big open windows that filled the space with great natural light. It made her small bedroom at home look like a broom closet.

A pretty, brunette saleswoman appeared and gave Emmie a bright smile. "I'm Hadlee and I'll be your personal shopper today." She turned to Dorian, "Why don't you have a seat while we work our magic. We'll take good care of her."

Hadlee ushered her into the huge fitting room, while Dorian settled himself on the sofa. She looked Emmie up and down.

"You're a size 14, right?"

Emmie blinked and her cheeks flamed as she nodded. "I don't know," she said, making eye contact with Hadlee in the mirror. "I don't think you'll have anything for me, that will,"—her gaze cut to the scar on her arm—"you know…look good on me." Her heart pounded, and she was beginning to feel light-headed. She hated this. Why had she agreed to come here?

"Nonsense," Hadlee said, smiling warmly at Emmie. "You have beautiful features and those eyes—" She rolled her eyes heavenward. "I think you need a cup of tea and while you're enjoying it, I'll make sure we find something that will make that gentleman out there speechless." She confirmed the rest of Emmie's sizes, then stepped out of the room for a moment before returning with an armful of gowns. A number of saleswomen followed, dropping off an assortment of shoes and underthings.

Emmie did most of her shopping online. There were no curious stares and awkward questions about her scars that way. No full length mirrors. Here, not only was she out of her element, but she was the center of attention with nearly the entire sales staff. She fought the urge to turn and run. Dorian went through a lot of extra trouble to make this happen, not to mention what her grandmother would say to her if she ran out.

Over the course of the next two hours, Emmie tried on more gowns than she could count, finally settling on a slate blue lace, off shoulder gown. The sleeves were just long enough to cover most of the scar on her arm and the fitted bodice hugged and streamlined her figure, along with a slightly flared maxi skirt and train. She couldn't believe the image blinking back at her in the mirror was actually her.

Hadlee helped her find the perfect pair of strappy heels to wear with the dress.

"Wear your hair up," Hadlee suggested. "You'll knock his socks off."

Emmie declined to let Dorian see her in the gown, opting instead to surprise him the next day. He had the boutique send the packages to the hotel and they walked a little farther down the street, stopping in front of a salon.

"You can't go to a ball without having a manicure," Dorian beamed. "I love your hair just as it is, but you are also free to have any of the salon services that you wish."

Emmie pressed her palms to her cheeks and slowly shook her head. She had to be dreaming. He didn't strike her as the kind of guy that would know much about manicures. "Do you have a secret life that I don't know about?"

Dorian chuckled and held his hands up in a 'you got me' gesture. "I called Anna," he confessed.

"She said to get you something called a mani pedi and asked me to tell you she thought you'd look amazing with some kind of caramel lights?" His brows furrowed and it was clear he had no idea what Anna told him had meant. "She suggested this place, so if you don't like it, you can blame her."

A wave of emotion coursed through her, growing with each beat of her heart. No one had ever done anything like this for her. "Dorian, I can't let you do this. The dress was so expensive and this,"— she waved her hand at the salon—"is just too much."

Dorian put his fingers under her chin and lifted it slightly, gazing into her eyes. "Let me do this, Em. Let me have this day with you."

Emmie thought for a minute. She'd never have the opportunity to experience something like this again. Not to mention she'd never be able to explain to her grandmother how she'd turned this down. And he *was* really sweet. "All right," she agreed, giving him a wide smile. "But we're going to do it my way."

DORIAN LOOKED DOWN AT his feet soaking in what he could only describe as a mini-Jacuzzi and wondered how he got talked into this. Trevor had secured the salon and made it clear in no uncertain terms that photos were not to be taken. He'd also made all of the technicians sign a non-disclosure form to prevent any media leaks, but Dorian still felt vulnerable and uncomfortable—yet, strangely relaxed at the same time. He could now understand why so many people did this. Emmie sat to his right, her feet soaking in her own mini-Jacuzzi. She met his gaze and grinned.

"Isn't this divine?" she asked with a half groan.

"It's...not bad," he hedged, not wanting to fully admit he was actually enjoying the experience. The chair was very plush and comfortable. He thought it resembled a modified recliner.

"Whatever," she said with a giggle. "You love it, and you know it."

"Maybe, but I'm drawing the line at polish," he laughed.

"Fine," she conceded with an exaggerated sigh, the corner of her mouth turned up. "You can be such an old fuddy-duddy."

"Fuddy-duddy?"

"Yes. Curmudgeon. Stuffed shirt. Mossback," she said with a chortle, her eyes sparkling with mischief. She was so cute when she was happy, and he loved how she teased him.

"I am *not* a stuffed shirt," he protested.

"Mmm-hmm," she teased.

A technician approached him and pulled a little remote-control unit from the back of his chair and handed it to him, explaining the buttons that would turn the chair into a massager. He pressed the buttons, testing how each worked and found a setting that had him taking a mental note to have a massage chair installed in his office at home, minus the foot Jacuzzi. Well, maybe with the foot Jacuzzi.

Several hours later, they emerged from the salon. Emmie's brown hair now had new caramel-colored highlights that gleamed in the sunshine. Anna was right about the extra color and Dorian noted an extra air of confidence about the way Emmie carried herself that wasn't there before. They both had hot pink nail polish on their toes and Dorian knew he'd have to give Trevor a handsome bonus to keep that information from being shared with the rest of the staff. But even he had to admit his feet felt better than they ever had.

They returned to the hotel and spent the rest of the evening playing a game called *Farkle* with the bodyguards. Emmie even talked Montgomery and Kate into playing. Dorian couldn't remember the last time he'd had that much fun, and he didn't think he'd ever seen Kate laugh so much. It was the best day he'd ever had. Emmie had introduced so many new and different things into his life in such a short time. He watched her laughing with Kate and his heart hurt knowing she'd be going back home soon.

How can I convince her to stay?

It was late and everyone was getting ready to turn in. Dorian walked Emmie to her room, and they stood in the doorway.

"Today was so much fun, Dorian." Emmie looked up at him, a wistful smile on her lips. "Thank you—for everything."

"It was," he agreed. "But I should be thanking you. So should my feet."

She smiled. "Especially your pink toes. You've set a new royal fashion statement."

Dorian chuckled softly. "I'm not so sure about that." He took a step closer to her. He loved the way the new highlights in her hair matched the honey color of her eyes. A flutter spread through his chest and a shiver ran down his spine.

"Emmie, you're so beautiful," he murmured, his voice husky.

"You are too," she whispered, then giggled nervously, her cheeks flushed.

Dorian's gaze slowly flickered from her eyes to her lips, then back up again. Her eyes were glossy and her lips slightly parted. He tried to calm his racing heart, but it was pointless. He *had* to kiss her. He brought his hand up and ran his fingers through the silky strands of her hair before he gently cupped the back of her head, his thumb gliding along her jaw. He leaned forward, tilting his head slightly, and then hesitated just inches from her face.

Emmie placed her hand on his chest, and he could feel the warmth from it spread through him. Her fingers curled into his shirt, and she gently pulled him to close the distance and pressed her lips to his. It was like no other kiss he'd ever had; it was...magic.

He lifted his hand to the small of her back and pulled her closer, pressing his lips to hers. Dorian lost all sense of where he was and the only thing he knew was that he never wanted this feeling to end.

Emmie abruptly pulled away, taking a step back from him, and folded her arms across her chest.

"Dorian, we can't—" she whispered, her breath quick and shallow.

Dorian's brain couldn't comprehend what she was saying. He *knew* she had kissed him back. Didn't she feel the same thing?

"I don't understand."

"Don't you see?" she pleaded, her eyes welling with tears. "We've gotten caught up in the moment. We can't do this. I'm leaving and you're going back to Avington. It's too hard." She backed into her room and closed the door.

"Emmie," he called, but there was no answer.

CHAPTER 17

Dorian slipped into his tuxedo jacket and adjusted his tie. The Animal Rescue Gala was a new event for him, but he was looking forward to bringing Emmie as his date. At least he assumed he was still bringing Emmie. He hadn't seen her since she retreated into her room after their earth-shattering kiss the night before. Dorian put his fingers to his lips. He could still feel the softness of her skin under his fingers and the sweet taste of her lips. Right now, he longed to be anything but a prince, so he'd have a real chance at having a relationship with her. Maybe tonight would change her mind. He checked his watch. It was nearly time to leave.

Dorian heard a door open, followed by the patter of little feet. Gatsby burst into his room fully decked out in his custom doggy tuxedo, complete with jacket and bowtie. Dorian took a treat off the dresser and crouched down to give it to the dog.

"Looking sharp there, Duke," he told Gatsby, patting him on the head. Gatsby wagged his tail, munched his tidbit and ran out of the room, his radar ears on full alert.

Dorian rose to his feet and followed him out. He froze mid-step when he saw her, his stomach erupting in a kaleidoscope of butterflies. The air rushed out of his lungs and he swore he could hear angels sing. Emmie wore a blue lace gown that hugged her curves without being provocative, like the dresses usually worn by other women he knew. Elegant was the word that came to mind. Her long, newly highlighted hair was piled high on her head with little ringlets falling around her face and neck, which was adorned with a simple silver chain. She wore very little makeup, but he never thought she needed it to begin with. No woman had ever looked so beautiful. He opened his mouth to speak but nothing came out.

Emmie's cheeks pinked and she gave Dorian a hint of a smile. "You look very handsome."

Dorian swallowed. "You're breathtaking."

Emmie's cheeks went from pink to bright red. "Thank you."

Dorian looked around to make sure they were alone. "Look, about last night—"

Kate rushed into the room and paused, thoroughly examining Emmie, before giving her a quick nod of approval. She turned to Dorian. "The car is here, Your Highness."

"We'll be right there," Dorian said, waving her on.

Kate's brow creased as her gaze flitted between him and Emmie. "Of course, Your Highness. We will be waiting."

As soon as Kate left the suite, Dorian turned back to Emmie. She had clipped a leash onto Gatsby's collar and carried a small black handbag.

"We can talk later. Let's not keep them waiting," she said and led Gatsby to the door.

They arrived at the gala and checked in at the registration table where they were provided with a list of auction items and directions to the silent auction tables. The attendant also told them where the reception would be held, as well as where they could find the Lucky Dog Lounge. They would be able to leave Gatsby there for thirty-minute intervals where he would be supervised and could play with the other dogs in attendance. Emmie pulled a copy of Gatsby's health records from her handbag and handed them to the attendant so they could get the collar tag for his access to the lounge. She then pointed them to a red-carpet photo booth and told them to have an enjoyable evening.

They posed for several photos with Gatsby at the photo booth and were told they could expect to receive prints within the week. Dorian put his hand on the small of Emmie's back and led her into the reception hall.

"Would you like a glass of wine?" he asked.

"I would love a glass, thank you."

"White or red?"

Emmie smiled. "Surprise me."

She looked radiant and Dorian was proud to have her as his date. He made his way to the bar and ordered two glasses of Pinot Grigio. He was waiting for them when someone tapped his shoulder. Turning, he was surprised to see Darcy Wallace, one of the few women NASCAR drivers. They'd met at a charity event in London the year before.

"Darcy, good to see you." Dorian leaned forward and air kissed her cheek. Looking down, he saw her corgi, Olive, who was wearing a dark green dress that matched Darcy's and a gold tiara. "Hey Olive," he greeted the dog.

"Prince Dorian," Darcy said with a smile. "Always good to see you." She glanced around with confusion. "Where is Gatsby?"

"He's with my date." Dorian gestured toward Emmie, who was busy talking to Gatsby.

Darcy looked surprised as she turned her attention to Emmie. "Is that Emmeline Walker?"

"Yes." Dorian was taken aback. "You *know* her?"

"No, not really," she replied. "One of my friends shows dogs and I saw her at Crestwood Hills. The corgi she was handling won best in show. My friend said she is one of the best handlers in the business, and one of the nicest people around. *She's* your date?"

Dorian flashed her a wide grin. "She is."

"There you are," a male voice came from behind Darcy and Dorian recognized Darcy's friend, Simon.

Simon scrutinized Dorian as a dark shadow crossed his face. "Prince Dorian," he said by way of greeting.

"Simon, good to see you again." Dorian nodded back and turned his attention back to Darcy. "I heard you retired. I'm going to miss watching you on the track." His mother may have banned racing from Avington, but Dorian loved watching NASCAR on TV.

"Thanks, it's different but it was time," she placed a hand on Simon's arm and gave him a loving glance. "We want to start a family."

"Congratulations," he said. "I'm happy for you both." Would he ever be able to say that? The urge to have a family of his own had never been so strong.

Simon cleared his throat. "We need to place our bid if you want to win," he gently reminded Darcy.

"Silent auction," Darcy laughed. "We'd better be going." She cut a glance to Emmie and leaned close to Dorian and murmured, "Hang on to that one, my friend. She's a keeper. Give Gatsby a kiss from Olive."

With a quick hug, she and Simon were gone.

"THANK YOU," EMMIE SAID, taking the glass of wine Dorian offered her. "Who was that at the bar?" Emmie thought the pretty brunette looked familiar but was unable to place her.

"Darcy Wallace. She just retired from NASCAR."

Emmie watched the handsome couple walk away. "Ahh, that's where I recognize her from. Do you know many people here?" She glanced around the room and recognized several celebrities. *What are you doing here? You do not fit in.*

Dorian scanned the crowd, subtly pointing to an attractive woman with long red hair. She had a corgi with her too and it was wearing a cute dress with a matching bow. "That's Julia Love. I know her."

"You *know* Julia Love? Oh my gosh, I love her cooking show. Gatsby and I were just watching it the other day."

Dorian took her elbow and gently nudged her forward. "Come, I'll introduce you."

Emmie walked with Dorian toward Julia feeling a little star struck and more than a little out of place.

"Prince Dorian! How wonderful to see you. It's been ages," Julia smiled.

"Julia, the pleasure is mine. I'd like you to meet my friend, Emmeline Walker."

Julia gave Emmie a warm smile. "Nice to meet you." She glanced down at the dog. "And there you are, Gatsby. I see you've found Penelope."

Emmie watched Gatsby and Penelope sniffing each other, tails wagging. She wasn't sure what to say and her hands were like icicles. "Hi," she finally managed. *Hi?* She felt like such a fool. She wasn't star struck by Dorian, but she'd been watching Julia Love for several years and admired her, not only for her cooking but her confidence.

"I'm sorry to have to run," Julia said, "but I need to check on the staff in the kitchen."

"You're catering this?" Dorian asked.

"I am," Julia replied and beamed with pride.

"What a treat," Emmie said, finding her voice.

"Thank you, Emmeline. I hope you enjoy it," Julia replied with a warm smile, then turned to Dorian. "Maybe I'll run into you later."

With a quick wave of her hand, Julia rushed off toward the Lucky Dog Lounge, where Emmie assumed she would drop off Penelope before she went into the kitchen.

"How do you know her?" Emmie asked, still trying to grasp the fact that she'd just had a conversation with one of her favorite celebrities.

"We've been at several of the same charity events. That's where I know most of these people from."

That made sense. Emmie glanced around the hall. There were vendor tables along one wall where the silent auction items were displayed. She recognized several of the vendors.

"Would you like to see what's on the silent auction tables?" Dorian asked. "I hope to find something I can bid on."

"That sounds good," Emmie answered. She wanted to look for something for her grandmother.

Dorian once again put his hand on the small of her back and walked with her toward the silent auction area. The heat of his touch sent tingles through her.

"Dorian," a familiar voice came from behind them. Emmie spun around and a sudden chill went through her.

"Ingrid," Dorian replied coldly. "What are you doing here?"

Ingrid smiled at him with feigned sweetness. "Darling, I'm here to see you, of course. And Gumby." She bent down to scratch Gatsby's head, but snatched her hand away when he growled. She straightened and flashed an accusing glare at Emmie. "I thought you were supposed to be a good dog trainer. He almost took my hand off."

"No such luck," Emmie mumbled.

Ingrid's eyes narrowed. "What did you say?"

"His name is Gatsby," Emmie said, slowly and deliberately.

Ingrid waved a manicured hand. "Whatever."

"Ingrid, *why* are you here?" Dorian cut in.

"Isn't it obvious?" She smoothed her hands along the curves of her form fitting black dress. "I'm your date."

Emmie felt her stomach lurch.

"I already *have* a date," Dorian said, his voice barely civil. A vein bulged on his forehead.

Ingrid cut a condescending glance at Emmie and laughed. "You can't be serious, Dorian. She's *the help*."

"She is my *date*, Ingrid. Something you will never be. Please leave."

"Don't be ridiculous, Dorian. You can't *date* the help. It's so beneath you." Ingrid lifted her chin and wrinkled her nose at Emmie's appearance. "Did you get that rag off the clearance rack? It's too bad you don't have a fairy godmother to fix it for you."

Emmie's nostrils flared with indignation. She knew better than to cause a scene at such a public event. She'd rather brush her teeth with a rock than let this...harpy ruin her night. "For your information, Dorian bought me this dress."

A flash of surprise crossed Ingrid's face, but just as quickly disappeared. "Of course, he did. It *is* a charity event after all."

"Ingrid," Dorian snapped. "That's quite enough."

"Dorian," Emmie said before Ingrid could say anything else. Placing her hand on Dorian's shoulder, she leaned toward him and handed him Gatsby's leash. "I'm going to run to the ladies' room while you sort this out." She brushed her lips against his cheek.

Ingrid's lips parted in shock and her face paled.

"Close your mouth, Ingrid, you look like a fish," Emmie scoffed as she walked away. Outwardly, she held her head high, but inside, her world turned grey.

Once inside the ladies' room, Emmie leaned against the sink and held a damp towel on the nape of her neck. *What were you thinking?* She'd deliberately provoked Ingrid by kissing Dorian's cheek, not to mention what kind of message it must have sent to him. And she was rude. Granted, Ingrid was awful, but she wasn't raised that way. *What would Nana say if she heard you?*

The door to the bathroom flew open and Ingrid burst into the room. Emmie straightened as Ingrid stopped in front of her. They stood close enough for her to see the pores on Ingrid's face. The stench of her perfume made Emmie take an instinctive step back.

Ingrid lifted her hand and pointed a long, perfectly manicured finger at Emmie. "You can play dress up all you want, but you'll never be good enough for him."

"It's *his* choice," Emmie shot back, but she knew what the other woman said was true. She was playing fairy tale, and nobody won that game.

"Why do you think I'm here?" she continued, her mouth twisted into a cruel sneer. "His *mother* sent me. You aren't what he needs, and she knows it too. As the queen, *she* has the final say. The Council would remove his title and he'd be a laughingstock. You'll ruin him if you continue this farce. Is that what you want?"

Emmie opened her mouth to argue that Ingrid was wrong, but nothing came out.

"I didn't think so," she said with a leer. And with that, Ingrid whirled around and strutted toward the door. She stopped with her hand on the door handle and looked over her shoulder at Emmie. "Besides, you'll never fit into his world, you know. You're nothing more than an indigent *dog trainer*," she said acidly and disappeared through the door.

Emmie gripped the sink, trying to collect herself. Ingrid might be rude, but she was right about one thing, Emmie would never fit in, and she wasn't about to put Dorian in a position where he had to choose between her or his family and his obligations. It was time to go home. She took a deep breath, smoothed the front of her dress with her hands and turned toward the door when she heard the chirp of her phone inside her handbag. She pulled it out and looked at the screen. It was the hospital. A sick feeling gripped her stomach.

"Hello?" she answered, her voice tentative.

"Emmeline, it's Agnes." The sound of Agnes sobbing on the other end of the phone made Emmie's whole body shake. "It's your grandmother. You need to come home."

CHAPTER 18

Dorian stood by the door to the ladies' room with Gatsby and waited for Emmie to come, hoping he didn't look like a stalker. He was still trying to figure out why Ingrid was there and the only answer he could come up with was that his mother had sent her. She'd made it perfectly clear over the years that she'd like nothing more than if Ingrid and he would pair off. It would never happen. Ingrid was nothing but an ill-mannered, spoiled brat.

The bathroom door opened, and Emmie flew out, tears streaming down her face. *What had Ingrid said to her?* Dorian rushed to her side, taking her hand in his to stop her. "Emmie, what happened? Are you all right?"

She looked at him with red-rimmed eyes and pulled her hand away. "Dorian, I'm sorry I need to go. Can you please take me back to the hotel, so I can get my things?" There was a different tone in her voice, almost like panic. She was almost running toward the exit. *She was leaving?*

Dorian hurried to catch up, oblivious to the glances of those around him. "Wait, what did she say to you, Emmie? You can't believe anything she says."

Emmie stopped and spun around with a pained look in her eyes. She was holding her hands together and he could see her rubbing her thumb against the palm of her hand. "It's not Ingrid," she said. The stress in her voice made his chest tighten. "It's my--my grandmother," Emmie choked out. "She's dying, Dorian. I need to go home. Now."

His mouth went dry. He bent down and scooped up Gatsby, tucking him under one arm, then he gripped Emmie's elbow and they rushed toward the exit. He signaled Brody, who'd been standing near the doors, to get the car.

Dorian watched helplessly as Emmie pulled her suitcase from her room. She had changed out of her gown into a pair of jeans and T-shirt. Her hair was pulled back into a ponytail. He had arranged for the car to take her to the airport. At least she'd agreed to that. He'd wanted to let her use the private jet, but she wouldn't have it.

Waiting silently, he watched as first Montgomery, then Kate, said their goodbyes. He was amazed when Kate reached out and gave Emmie's hand a squeeze. Emmie's magic touched everyone around her. She knelt next to Gatsby, gathered him into her arms and gave him a long hug.

"Oh Duke, I will miss you," Emmie said into his fur. "You be a good boy for Dad, all right?" A tear ran down her face. "I'll miss you so much," she said and kissed Gatsby several times on his furry head before she placed him back on the floor.

When it was Dorian's turn, his stomach twisted at the prospect of her leaving. Would she ever come back to him? The sadness in her eyes was almost more than he could bear.

"Montgomery assured me he'd help you get Gatsby home in one piece," she said with a half-smile and wiped a tear from her cheek.

"You need to be with her, I understand. Montgomery will take care of your remaining compensation. You should have it in a couple of days. You'll let me know if you need anything, right? Anything at all."

Emmie chewed on her bottom lip but didn't answer him.

"Will I see you again?" he asked, his voice low. He studied her face, waiting for her to answer, trying to memorize every detail.

"I don't think so," she whispered, her gaze shifting to the floor.

It was as though someone had reached into his chest and ripped out his heart. "Please, Emmie. There's something between us, don't you feel it?"

She took a deep breath and exhaled slowly before looking up, her eyes pooled with tears. "It doesn't matter how I feel, Dorian. It won't work between us. We come from two different worlds."

He reached for her hand. "But it *does* matter. I care about you, and I am pretty sure you feel the same way about me."

Emmie pulled her hand away. "Don't you see?" she cried, her voice breaking. "I will never fit in. They'll never accept me. I can't do that to you."

"But—"

She put her finger on his lips. "Don't Dorian, please. Just let it go. You'll go back to Avington and forget all about me." She reached for the handle of her suitcase, her chin quivering. "I have to go.

The car is waiting." She rose up on her toes, placed a soft kiss on his cheek, then walked to the door. She stopped in the doorway. "I'll never forget you," she said as tears streamed down her face. She went through the door, and he watched it close, the click of the latch echoing in the empty room.

His chest became heavy, and his pulse raced. He breathed in, but it was like it was the wrong kind of air and his lungs wouldn't fill. He stared at the door, praying for it to open. He wanted Emmie to rush back in to tell him she wanted him, but it stayed shut. Gatsby whined at his feet. Dorian looked down at the dog, who also stared at the door.

What if you never see her again?

The thought was more than he could bear. He loved her. The realization hit him so unexpectedly and with such force, he had to stifle a gasp. *He loved her.* He had to tell her before he lost his chance, or his nerve.

He rushed out the door. "Emmie, wait!" Dorian pushed the elevator button frantically, as if that might make the doors open sooner. They finally slid open and he stepped in just as Brody rushed out of the suite. Their eyes locked as the doors closed leaving the bodyguard on the outside. After what seemed like forever, Dorian burst out of the elevator into the lobby and caught a glimpse of Emmie entering the large revolving door at the hotel entrance.

"Emmie!" he called, but she didn't hear him. He sprinted across the hotel lobby, dodged a porter and almost ran into an elderly man who had stooped to pick up a dropped coin. He didn't want to waste time in the slow-moving revolving door, so he pushed open the large, glass exit door situated to the left of it. As he passed through it, he heard someone shout, "There he is! It's Prince Dorian!"

Cameras flashed, and he saw a news crew and reporters closing in on him. They must have camped out there since last night. Dorian knew his location had been compromised with their abrupt departure from the gala. They followed him and they wanted "a story". His gaze darted through the crowd, frantically hunting for any sign of Emmie. He spotted her at the curb, about to step into the waiting car.

"Emmie, wait!" He pushed his way toward her. He could hear Brody, Chet and Trevor moving through the crowd behind him. "Emmie!" he called again. She paused. The door to the car was open and the driver was loading her luggage into the trunk. As their gazes met, Dorian no longer heard the questions the reporters were throwing at him, or the click of cameras going off around him. All he saw was Emmie and all he wanted to do was hold her and never let her go.

"Dorian," she said as he approached, surprise and sadness in her voice. "What are you doing here?"

"Emmie," he said breathlessly, "I can't let you leave without telling you what's in my heart." Bracing himself with one hand on the top of the open door and one on the roof of the car, he leaned forward to murmur in her ear. "I'm in love with you." *There. He'd said it.* He pulled back to look into her eyes. "I love you. Please come back to me."

She froze, unable to speak, but her eyes were filled with longing.

He moved closer, his heart pounding with the realization that he was going to kiss her. He desperately needed to kiss her—here, now. Emmie couldn't leave without knowing how much he cared about her and how much he wanted her to return to him as soon as she could.

It didn't matter who saw them. He didn't care about anything but her. This was his only chance to prove to her his love was real. Pulling her into his arms, he lowered his mouth to hers. The sensation was dizzying, an exhilaration he never knew existed.

One he craved again and again, only with her. He kissed her with all the pent up desire he had since they met. His boldness caused her to hesitate, but only briefly before she slid her arms around his neck and kissed him back.

The kiss grew more fervent, more demanding until she pulled back, both of them breathless. She put her palms on his chest and pushed him away, shaking her head violently. "Dorian, please. Don't. I want this as much as you do, but it's impossible. I can't. We can't." Emmie began to sob, "I'm so sorry."

Turning away before he could respond, she slipped into the car and slammed the door shut.

Her rejection pierced like a knife to his heart.

Brody's wide hand gripped his arm, pulling him to safety as he watched the vehicle drive away with the only woman he'd ever loved, and his happiness.

Emmie sat in the back seat of the car with her hands over her eyes and sobbed. The hurt and rejection on Dorian's face when she pulled away from their kiss would be etched in her mind forever.

He told you he was in love with you. Why didn't you tell him you loved him too?

Emmie pushed that thought from her mind. It didn't matter. The queen would never accept her; that was made perfectly clear. If she came back, it would only cause a rift between Dorian and his family, and she didn't want to be a divider. If what Ingrid said about the Council stripping him of his title was true, she'd never be able to live with herself if he estranged himself from his family because of her.

Would she ever be able to un-see the haunted look in his eyes? She hadn't meant to hurt him. Hadn't meant to fall in love with him. Hadn't meant for any of this to happen.

Her throat constricted, and a vice closed around her chest, making it hard to breathe. She was losing everyone she loved. Emmie wiped her eyes and took several deep breaths. She needed to hold it together for her grandmother right now. She could only hope she'd make it home in time.

Emmie caught a direct flight from Los Angeles to Minneapolis. She tried to sleep on the three-and-a-half-hour flight, but intertwining thoughts of Dorian and her grandmother wouldn't allow for it. So, she prayed instead. Prayed for her grandmother. Prayed for Dorian. Prayed for herself. By the time the plane touched down, a strange sense of peace settled over her. A familiar portion of a Bible verse came to mind, *To every thing there is a season, and a time to every purpose under the heaven.*

Emmie's stomach churned as she walked down the brightly lit hallway of Grace Hospital, her footsteps echoing on the tile floor. The acrid smell of astringent filled her nose, and a cacophony of sounds filled her ears as she walked past patient rooms and the nurses' station. She paused outside the door to her grandmother's room, her thumb rubbing against the palm of her opposite hand in a soothing motion.

Will she know I'm here and who I am? Will she be able to speak? Please God, let her know I'm here.

Emmie took a few calming breaths and pulled open the door. The sickeningly sweet smell of lilies hit her first. Her grandmother loved lilies. An array of cards and brightly colored predominantly lily floral arrangements lined the shelf below the large window. The blinds were closed and a fluorescent light glowed over the bed where a still figure lay. A heart monitor beeped on one side of the bed and several bags of fluids hung from a metal IV pole on the other side. A woman with light blue hair and a bright hibiscus patterned dress slumped in a chair next to the bed, snoring softly. *Agnes.*

She stepped next to the bed and barely recognized the frail, grey-haired woman that lay in it, an oxygen tube in her nose and a blood pressure cuff wrapped around one arm. Emmie had tried to mentally prepare herself, but to see her grandmother like this was shocking and difficult. She'd always been the strong one. The take-charge, get things done kind of person. Emmie reached out and curled her fingers around her grandmother's hand. It was cold and motionless.

"Nana, I'm here," Emmie said softly, leaning forward and pressing her lips to her grandmother's cheek. She didn't get any response. A tightness settled in her chest and her throat constricted.

Agnes stirred and sat up. It took her a moment to recognize Emmie, but when she did, she leapt up and rushed around the bed to throw her arms around Emmie.

Her grandmother and Agnes had met when Agnes moved into the apartment next door to her grandmother's in the assisted living center. Though her grandmother already had a lot of friends, she and Agnes had become very close, and Emmie was grateful for Agnes's loyalty and the companionship she'd given her grandmother these last few weeks.

"Oh honey, I'm so glad you're here." Agnes pulled away and dabbed at her eyes with a tie-dyed handkerchief. "It happened so fast." Agnes sniffed and gazed lovingly at Blanche. "We couldn't get her to eat anything, and then she was in so much pain they kept giving her more morphine. I told them she was going to become an addict, but they just kept giving her more. Said it didn't matter if she...she got addicted." Agnes' voice broke and she closed her eyes, struggling to hold back her grief.

Emmie gently touched Agnes' arm and gave it a light squeeze.

"Then...then she just didn't wake up," Agnes said and sniffed again. "It was so fast." Agnes stared at Blanche. "She's my friend," she said softly. "My best friend."

Tears welled up in Emmie's eyes and overflowed to streak down her face and onto her collarbone. She reached for a tissue from the box on the nightstand and swiped them away.

"You're *her* best friend too," Emmie choked out.

Agnes covered Emmie's hand with her own. "I'm going to go get me some coffee; so you sit with her and have some time alone. That new doctor did say she could wake up, but he didn't know if she would."

Emmie nodded. "Okay. Thank you, Agnes," she managed to say. "Thank you for everything." She waited until Agnes had left the room before she walked to the other side of the bed and sank into the chair Agnes had been resting in. Her limbs were numb and weak.

Emmie found herself wishing Dorian were here to help her, to hold her like he had the night of the storm. Her grandmother lay still, her breathing shallow. Emmie leaned forward until her forehead rested on the bed by her grandmother's arm and the tears she'd been fighting so hard to hold off refused to be denied, and her whole body shook.

A slight pressure of what felt like fingers touching her head woke her. She bolted upright.

Her grandmother's arm fell back to her side. Her rheumy eyes staring into Emmie's.

She was awake, she was awake!

"Nana," Emmie cried. "Nana, I'm here."

"Emmie..." her grandmother's voice was hoarse and weak.

"Do you want some water?"

Her grandmother gave a nearly imperceptible shake of her head. She moved her arm so her hand was holding Emmie's and she gave it a weak squeeze. Her eyes rolled and struggled to focus, finally settling on Emmie.

"Where is your prince?" she croaked.

Emmie's stomach plummeted. "Nana, he's not my prince," she answered, unable to keep the sadness from her voice. "There are so many things I want to say to you—"

"Where is your prince?" her grandmother asked more forcefully.

Did she understand what was being said? Emmie looked at her carefully. "Nana, he went home. He's not with me."

"Why?"

"Because..." Emmie bit her lip and tried to find the right words to make her understand. "We're from two different worlds, Nana. It can't work."

Her grandmother shook her head and swallowed hard. Her eyes closed once again.

No, don't leave me yet!

Emmie gently squeezed her grandmother's hand and her eyes fluttered open again. She looked more alert.

"You're a good girl, Emmie," she whispered. Emmie leaned closer so she could hear easier. "Don't shut people out. You have a lot to give."

Emmie's eyebrows scrunched with pain. Her eyes and nose tingled as her eyes once again smarted with tears. "Nana—" she began but her grandmother lifted a tired finger to stop her.

"He will adjust his world so you fit. You belong with him." Her grandmother's eyes were struggling to stay open. "They told me," she whispered.

"Who did?"

"Your guardian angels."

"Angels?"

Her grandmother nodded her head. "Be good to him, Emmie. Promise me," she said weakly.

The tears were now freely flowing down Emmie's face. "Nana, no. I need more time."

"Promise me, Emmie."

"I promise," Emmie sobbed.

"I love you, sweet girl. Remember to listen to the angels." Her words ended in a fit of coughing that left her pale and shaking.

"Nana, I'm scared."

"Don't be afraid, Em. Remember when fear knocks on your door, you need to send faith to answer. Never lose your faith and you'll be just fine." She closed her eyes and let out a long breath.

"I love you, Nana. I love you so much." Emmie waited to see if her grandmother would open her eyes again, but she didn't. "Nana?" She could see the slight rise and fall of her grandmother's chest and the heart monitor beep was steady. She gently shook her grandmother's arm. "Nana?" Getting no response, Emmie picked up her grandmother's hand and held it to her lips and prayed.

Her grandmother never reawakened. Emmie and Agnes kept a vigil by her bedside for three more days before the heart monitor stopped beeping, the zig-zag on the screen turned into a flat line. Emmie watched in disbelief as the nurses gently disconnected the heart monitor and removed the IV from her arm. One of them touched Emmie's shoulder on her way out of the room, but she barely felt it. She didn't feel anything. A weight settled on her heart. She was now all alone in the world. Her worst nightmare had come true. Everyone she had ever loved was gone.

Her phone buzzed in her pocket. She pulled it out and looked at the screen. It was Dorian.

CHAPTER 19

Dorian had been back in Avington for over a week and was still unable to get Emmie off his mind. He'd spent a small part of that time setting up an advisory board for Ava's Angels. While he'd been excited to get that closer to going public, right now, he was just going through the motions. He'd done nothing with all of the ideas he'd come up with while in America either.

He just couldn't get motivated to do anything but think about Emmie. He'd tried calling her several times, but she never answered. Each time he'd tried, he held his breath in anticipation of hearing her voice on the other end of the line, and each time she didn't, he felt another piece of his heart break.

Dorian canceled all of his meetings and took to spending his time in his suite of rooms at the castle, alone with Gatsby, eating ice cream and watching movies. He must have watched *Pretty Woman* at least a half a dozen times. Remnants of hot pink nail polish could still be seen on his toes. He'd considered trying to remove it, but it was the only thing left he had of her. He had even tried to get the royal chef to make a version of a Mac Daddy-O, but it wasn't the same and the sorry imitation only served to darken his mood even more. Nothing was right without Emmie.

He settled onto the couch in his suite and paged through a list of movies, finally selecting *Titanic*. A movie where nearly everyone died at the end somehow seemed fitting, given his current mood. Happy endings only happened in fairy tales. Gatsby, who had been sleeping, now sat alert, his ears pointed toward the door. Seconds later, there was a soft knock.

Dorian didn't want company. "Go away," he said, his voice gravelly from lack of sleep. The knock sounded again. Dorian's muscles tensed with anger. "I said, go away!" The persistent rapping continued and Dorian heard Montgomery's voice on the other side of the door.

"Your Highness, I *must* speak with you."

This had better be good.

Dorian swung his legs onto the floor and was across the room in four strides. He turned the lock and yanked the door open. "What?"

Montgomery's gaze raked over Dorian's disheveled appearance. Looking past Dorian's shoulder, he quickly scanned the room. Empty ice cream cartons and a half-eaten sandwich were strewn across the mahogany coffee table. Dorian hadn't even allowed the cleaning staff into his chambers.

"Your Highness, I apologize for the interruption, but Her Majesty has returned and is requesting your presence. Immediately."

Dorian hadn't been able to confront his mother since his return, as she had been on holiday with her friend, Leticia. He'd forgotten she was due back today. His stomach roiled. He didn't want to deal with her right now, but knew he had no choice. When you were summoned by the queen, you showed up.

"I also thought you might like these. They came in today's post." Montgomery handed Dorian a large envelope.

Dorian undid the clasp and pulled out several photos in various sizes. They were the pictures of him and Emmie from the photo booth at the gala. His arms grew heavy as he sifted through them. Emmie looked absolutely stunning next to him and Gatsby. Her smile was radiant. In one of the photos, they were looking at each other as if they had just shared some secret between them. A knife of pain twisted in his heart. He ran his hand through his hair and his throat constricted. Shoving the photos back into the envelope, he set it on the side table by the door and took a deep breath. *Might as well get this over with*, he thought as he moved to pass Montgomery.

"If I may, Your Highness," Montgomery said, looking Dorian in the eye. "You might consider a change of clothing before you have your audience with Her Majesty...and perhaps a shower?"

Dorian glanced at the faded blue jeans and T-shirt he wore. It was the outfit Emmie had picked out for him the afternoon they'd spent together on Beale Street in Memphis. He'd been wearing the ensemble all week. The shirt was stained and wrinkled, probably smelled. He didn't care. *Would he ever see her again?* Dorian felt hollow inside.

"Tell her I'll be there after I shower," he said with resignation in his voice.

"Yes, Your Highness," Montgomery said. He paused for a moment, then continued. "Emmie was quite fetching in that gown."

Dorian's gaze took in the wistful expression on Montgomery's face. He nodded in agreement.

"At the risk of being improper, may I speak candidly with you?"

Surprised, Dorian raised an eyebrow. Montgomery had often given him advice throughout the years and had become a trusted confidant, but he had never asked to speak *candidly* with him. "Of course."

Montgomery cleared his throat and loosened his collar with one finger before he spoke. "She was good for you, Dorian. You were good together. I wouldn't be so quick to let her go." He pulled a folded piece of paper from his pocket and handed it to Dorian, then slipped out the door.

Dorian unfolded the paper and stared at the words. It was Emmie's address in Minnesota.

Freshly showered, Dorian walked through the ornate halls of Dorburn toward his mother's study. Behind him, Gatsby's nails made little clicking sounds on the tile floor. As he approached the door, he heard footfalls behind him and turned. It was Ingrid.

"There you are," she said, her voice a sexy purr.

"Ingrid, *what* are you doing here?" Dorian didn't even bother to hide his frustration and loathing at her presence.

Ingrid sidled up next to him and placed her palm on his chest. "Now that you've come to your senses and that awful American pauper is out of the way, there's nothing stopping us from being together."

Dorian couldn't believe his ears. Irritated, he pushed her hand away. "How many times do I need to tell you, Ingrid? We will *never* be together. And don't you ever talk about Emmie in that way again. She may not have a title, but she has more grace and style than you will ever have."

Ingrid sniffed with a dismissive wave. "Even your mother wants us to be together."

"What gives you that idea?" Dorian snapped in denial, even though his mother had been pushing him toward Ingrid for years.

"Why do you think I was at the gala? It certainly wasn't to save the animals."

Dorian fought to keep his expression neutral, but this confirmed suspicions about Ingrid's presence there. "You may have her fooled with your princess act, but I see right through you."

"Oh, you miss her, don't you? How sweet," Ingrid asked, sarcasm dripping from her voice. She folded her arms across her chest and lifted her chin. "She'll never be yours, Dorian."

"That isn't your decision to make, Ingrid," Dorian said through clenched teeth.

"It's not yours either," she said with a chortle, her lips curving into a wicked, knowing smile. "You know as well as I do that the Queen must give her approval. I made sure your precious *dog trainer* knew that too."

The muscles in his jaw tightened and sweat collected under his collar. "What do you mean?" he asked through clenched teeth.

Ingrid, oblivious to his anger, smiled like a proud child. "It was nothing," she replied with an indifferent shrug. "I simply pointed out that you'd lose your crown and your family if she insisted on staying."

What? A conflicting combination of rage and relief washed over him as he realized Emmie didn't leave because she didn't want him. She left because she was trying to *protect* him. He bore down on

Ingrid with a hard, unyielding stare. "Leave," he snarled. "Get out of my sight. *Now.*"

Ingrid's eyes went wide. "But Dorian, don't you see? We—"

"There is no *we*," he roared. "There will *never* be a *we*. Get it through your head, Ingrid."

"I am a princess, and don't you forget it. No one tells me no. Including you." She pointed a brightly polished nail at his chest. "You wait, Dorian Tennesley. You wait until I get through with you in the press. I'll make what that actress made up about you look like child's play."

"You will do no such thing," Sophia declared.

Dorian spun toward his mother's voice. She stood in the doorway of her study, her face flushed, her eyes cold and hard. He hadn't heard her come out and clearly, neither had Ingrid. Dorian saw the color leave Ingrid's face and he couldn't hold back a triumphant smile.

"Your Majesty, I was—"

"I know exactly what you were doing," Sophia said, moving out from behind Dorian to stand in front of Ingrid. Out of the corner of his eye, Dorian saw Ingrid's mother, Lady Leticia, follow, her face a bright shade of red.

"Ingrid, it's only because of my friendship with your mother that I am refraining from having you brought up on charges of attempted slander against a member of the royal family."

Ingrid's face blanched. "But—"

"Enough!"

Dorian's mouth fell open. He had never heard his mother raise her voice. Ever.

"You are no longer welcome at Dorburn. If I see or hear that you are on the grounds again, I will make sure you are brought up on charges before the Council."

Ingrid opened her mouth as if to speak but was interrupted by her mother.

"That's quite enough, Ingrid," Leticia admonished her daughter. "Now see what your impertinence has cost you? You're an embarrassment to the family." She turned to the prince, her eyes cast down. "I'm so very sorry, Dorian."

Dorian didn't know what to say. He held no ill will toward Ingrid's mother, other than wishing she had perhaps exercised better judgement and not coddled her daughter so much. But he also knew the sins of the child were not the fault of the parent. He simply gave a nod acknowledging her apology.

Sophia put her hand on Leticia's arm and gave it a gentle rub. "We will reconvene our luncheon date tomorrow." She smiled kindly at her friend.

Leticia grabbed Ingrid by the arm and led her away. Dorian heard their hushed bickering as they disappeared down the stairs. As he turned back to his mother, he noticed a sadness clouding her features. She motioned toward her study. "Let's talk, shall we?"

They settled on the long, ivory sofa. She took his hands in hers and gazed at him solemnly. "I believe I owe you an apology," she said. "I let my friendship with Leticia cloud my vision of who Ingrid really is." She pulled her hands back and folded them in her lap.

Dorian blinked, not sure what to say. He reached forward and gave her hand a gentle squeeze. He believed her heart had been in the right place, but her actions had precipitated the events that led to his losing Emmie.

Sophia grimaced. "I have made quite a mess of things for you."

"You might say that."

"I'm sorry, Dorian."

They sat in awkward silence for a few minutes. "I hear you have been despondent since your return from America."

Dorian shrugged. He didn't care to discuss his feelings with his mother. How could she relate?

"Kate also mentioned that you canceled all your meetings, except those involving some charity you are setting up. You haven't told me about that."

Dorian met her gaze. He had been wanting to surprise her with that information once the charity was fully operational, but decided now was as good a time as any to share it with her.

"It's called *Ava's Angels.*"

Sophia gasped and put her hand over her mouth. Her eyes glazed with tears.

"The purpose will be to help families with sick children, so they can afford to take time off work to take care of their families without having to worry about bills. I wanted to do something special in Ava's name, something meaningful."

"Oh Dorian," Sophia cried and pulled him into a hug. "I have underestimated you too. When Ava died, a part of me died too. Her life was so short. She never had a chance to live her dreams. But now, her life has a purpose. You've given her that. Thank you, son." She sobbed quietly into his shoulder for a few minutes before pulling back. She wiped under her eyes and patted her hair back in place. Always the queen.

"This girl, Emmie. She is important to you, isn't she?"

Dorian nodded. "I've never met anyone like her."

"Neither have I," she said with a chuckle. "The press seems to love her too, despite my best efforts to avoid that." She gave Dorian a meaningful glance, but he knew she meant no malice. Sophia's gaze shifted to the large window on the far end of her study. Dorian knew what she was seeing was not to be found on the other side of the glass pane.

"Many years ago, I met a young man," she began. A flush of pink colored her cheeks. "I've never told anyone this before. Well, except Leticia, but she was there."

Intrigued, Dorian leaned forward.

"Leticia and I were young women, girls really, and we had been allowed to go into the city to get the new Beatles record," she snorted. The corners of her mouth turned up in a wistful smile. "We stopped for ice cream on the way home…"

Dorian froze at his mother's admission. He'd never seen her indulge in ice cream and he thought she hated the Beatles. Sophia noticed his reaction and smiled. "Yes, ice cream. I used to love it," she said, the faraway look returning to her eyes. "There was a young man working behind the counter. He was so dreamy," she said and sighed.

Dreamy?

"He reminded me of that American actor, James Dean. Anyway, we fell in love…or at least what my young heart thought was love."

She had been in love with a civilian? Dorian was astonished.

"Oh, but I was a fool for that boy," she went on. "Until my father found out." The dreamy expression left his mother's face, replaced with sadness. "He forbade me from ever seeing the young man again, even going so far as to arrange my marriage to your father."

What? They had an arranged marriage? How did he know so little about his mother? "I never knew—" he began but she waved him off.

"No one knew. We were able to keep that particular piece of information out of the press. We eventually grew to appreciate one another and that ultimately turned to its own kind of love." She looked at Dorian intently. "I loved your father. I did. I was devastated when he was killed." Dorian could see tears welling in her eyes.

"I know you did, Mother."

She gave him a gracious smile and the faraway look returned to her eyes. "But I always wondered what would have happened if Father hadn't--" She shook her head and rose to her feet, smoothing her white linen pants with her hands as she walked to the window. "It doesn't matter anymore. Not for me. But it does for you." She turned and returned to where Dorian was now standing.

"What are you saying?" His eyes searched hers, looking for an answer.

"Are you in love with her?"

"We've known each other for such a short time, but I feel different when I'm with her. I feel..." Dorian paused while he searched for the right word.

"Complete."

"Complete. I do love her, Mother."

They stood, facing each other and she took his hands in hers. "Ever since you were a little boy, you have been envious of Philip's eventual taking of the throne."

Dorian opened his mouth to protest but closed it. There was some truth to that, perhaps less now though.

"You don't know what a gift that is, Dorian, that you will not wear the crown. That gives you the freedom to choose. I have been a selfish woman, trying to impose tradition upon you. That will end here. From now on, you choose. Let your heart choose. I believe when you find what your grandmother used to call your *other half*, the stars align, and it just happens. It's like—"

"Magic," they said together.

"Mother—"

"Go son. Go get your princess."

Dorian pulled her into a warm hug, then stepped away. His heart hammered as he dug his phone from his pocket. He dialed a number and waited until he heard someone pick up on the other end.

"I need to file a flight plan."

CHAPTER 20

Emmie stood in the private family room of the funeral home, trying compose herself before she joined her grandmother's friends in the reception room. She dug through the tote bag she'd brought with her change of clothing and pulled out Charlie. The bear had become a source of comfort to her these last few days.

It had been raining when she left the apartment, aptly so, and she had opted to change into her funeral dress here. Gazing out the window, she noticed that the sky had now cleared and was a vibrant blue with white puffs of clouds scattered aimlessly across it. She sank into one of the two plush chairs in the room, held Charlie close to her chest, and tried to focus on the soothing music coming from the speakers nestled into the ceiling tiles. She still couldn't believe Nana was gone.

Emmie moved Charlie to her lap and sighed. Her fingers ran along the red bow tied around the bear's neck. *Charlie makes me feel better when I get sad about my scars*, she remembered the little girl, Daisy, telling her at the Children's Hospital when she gave Emmie the bear. *But what about the scars inside?*

The past few days had been a whirlwind of activity. Emmie and Agnes worked with the funeral director to plan her grandmother's funeral. She'd also met with her grandmother's attorney to review the will. As expected, her entire estate, which consisted of a modest life insurance policy and her personal property, was left to Emmie.

Emmie was grateful for the life insurance policy, as it would give her enough money to pay off the hospital bill and funeral expenses. With what was left, plus the generous payment she'd received from Montgomery, she would be able to start working on a business plan for the dog training facility.

Was it still what she wanted? She didn't know. Nothing appealed to her right now. She was living from day to day, struggling to deal with the loss of the two most important people in her life—Nana and Dorian.

Dorian's smiling face penetrated her thoughts, causing an immediate thickening in her throat. He had tried calling her a number of times throughout the week, but she hadn't answered any of the calls. It was better this way, wasn't it? She hadn't been able to stop thinking about him and what Nana had said to her. That the angels told her they belonged together. It was an odd thing for her to have said and at the time, Emmie had dismissed it as a by-product from the fog caused by the strong painkillers she had been given. Now, the words haunted her. *What if they did belong together?*

No. She rose to her feet and tucked Charlie back into her tote. She had to stop thinking about Dorian. And Gatsby. Even so, the thought of never seeing them again made tears well in her eyes. The room became blurry. She pulled a tissue from the box on the table and dabbed at the corners of her eyes until the room became clear once again. She had done the right thing by telling him goodbye, no matter how wrong it felt. She couldn't be responsible for causing a falling out between him and his family. She knew what it was like to have no family and she wasn't going to do that to him. Emmie took a deep cleansing breath, squared her shoulders, and stepped out of the room into the reception hall.

The tables were full of people who had come to pay their last respects to Blanche. The murmur of their conversations created a continuous din that drowned out the classical music that played through the ceiling speakers. Emmie had lived in this small community nearly her entire life and she wondered if perhaps the entire town had shown up.

A line formed at the buffet table where people filled their plates with potato salad and finger sandwiches. The thought of eating potato salad made Emmie's stomach turn, even though she normally loved it. Nothing tasted right anymore.

"Emmeline! There you are!" Agnes's familiar voice rose above the chatter in the room. Emmie turned to see Agnes rushing toward her. She had swapped her usual bright floral print dress for a plain black one adorned with white tropical flowers. Her salon-styled hair was now cotton-candy pink and lacquered so stiff it looked like a wig. Agnes stopped in front of Emmie, her normally small eyes now big and round, her face flushed a dark red.

"Oh, my stars and garters!" Agnes pressed a hand to her chest, trying to catch her breath.

Puzzled, Emmie glanced around the room and tried to figure out what had the older woman so wound up.

"Emmeline, you *have* to come outside, right now!" Agnes grabbed Emmie's hand and pulled her toward the exit.

"What is it, Agnes? What's wrong?"

"Nothing's wrong, silly girl. Everything is turning out the way God intended all along. He's here." She stopped and pumped Emmie's arm up and down, a gleeful expression on her face. "Your prince. He's here!"

"W-w-what?" she stammered. *Dorian? He's here?* No, Agnes must be confused. Dorian was in Avington.

"Outside," Agnes beamed and pointed to the door. "Oh honey, he's here and he is hotter than a rabbit's butt in a pepper patch." Agnes gave Emmie a conspiratorial wink along with a slight shove toward the door. "Go on now before I decide to impersonate you and go after him myself."

Emmie's heart slammed in her chest, threatening to burst at any moment. She grasped the door handle with a shaky hand and pulled it open. Her breath caught in her throat.

A glossy white limousine was parked directly across the street from the entrance to the funeral home. Leaning casually against it with his long legs crossed at the ankles, stood Dorian. He wore mirrored sunglasses and a familiar pair of faded jeans and a hockey T-shirt. Gatsby and Brody stood alongside him. He held a pint of ice cream in one hand and Gatsby's leash in the other. The brisk breeze tousled his wavy, dark hair, and he had a day's worth of stubble along his chin and jaw. A smile tugged at his lips.

As long as she lived, she'd never behold a man that looked more attractive than he did in that moment.

She took a tentative step toward him, her knees weakening and her stomach in a constant flutter.

Gatsby recognized her and yipped with excitement, pulling at his leash. Dorian murmured something unintelligible to the dog, and he quieted. Dorian pulled his sunglasses off, then straightened and handed them, along with Gatsby's leash and the ice cream to Brody. With three long strides, he closed the distance between them.

"It's not quite a white horse," Dorian gestured toward the limo, "but it is white. And I don't have a sword to draw, but I did bring ice cream." He gave her a loving smile, his dazzling blue eyes locking on hers. She was momentarily confused but then it clicked, and tears threatened to spill from her eyes. It was from the end of *Pretty Woman*.

"Are you here to rescue me?" Emmie asked breathlessly.

"No," Dorian said as he wrapped his arms around her. "I'm here so you can rescue me."

EPILOGUE

One Year Later

Philip adjusted the purple sash that went across the bright red Queen's Guard uniform Dorian wore, then clapped him on the shoulder.

"Are you ready?" he asked.

In the last year, Dorian's relationship with his brother had changed by leaps and bounds. With the establishment of Ava's Angels, and the support of their mother, the two brothers had finally found common ground. Anna and Emmie had become close over the course of the year as well, and the four of them could be found together quite often.

Emmie. It hadn't taken Dorian long to smooth things over when he showed up at her grandmother's funeral in Minnesota. To his relief, she had agreed to give their relationship a chance. Emmie had stayed behind in Minnesota for a couple of weeks after that to finalize her grandmother's estate and clean out the apartment they had once shared. She had been given a suite in the guest wing of the castle upon her arrival in Avington. It hadn't taken long before she'd captured the hearts of everyone around her, most importantly his.

Emmie and Anna, with Dorian's help, worked together to create a charity and dog training facility called *PawsUp*. They worked with animal rescue organizations throughout the world to bring rescue dogs to the training facility to be trained as emotional support and service animals to be given to veterans at no cost. It garnered a huge amount of publicity and as a result, the tourism industry in Avington was now thriving as well.

Sophia, once the initial awkwardness between them passed, had taken Emmie under her wing. It was not unusual for them to be seen shopping together or going to visit the sick children at Avington Children's Hospital together, bringing them books and toys and letting them play with Gatsby.

Dorian asked Emmie to be his wife on Christmas Eve of that year. Sophia had given him a diamond and sapphire ring that had belonged to his grandmother, along with her blessing. He carefully tied the ring to Gatsby's collar with a tag that read *Will you marry us?* and had Gatsby sit under the elaborately decorated Christmas tree. Philip brought Emmie into the room, and they all watched as she first saw the ring on Gatsby's neck and then Dorian on a bended knee. The press had loved the story and they had been the world's most watched couple ever since.

Philip's hand pressed upon his shoulder again, this time giving him a gentle shake. "Are you ready?" Philip asked again, bringing Dorian out of his reverie. "She's on her way."

Dorian felt what he could only describe as butterflies in his stomach as he walked with Philip into the full chapel to stand at the altar. The only decoration was a stunning arrangement of white roses, red carnations and white button chrysanthemums. Nestled in between the flowers were two crystal cardinal figurines. One for Blanche, the other for Ava. A long red carpet ran the length of the chapel down the center aisle. The children from the Avington Children's Choir were in the choir loft and had just finished singing a hauntingly beautiful version of *Ave Maria*.

Dorian's gaze flitted through the crowded chapel. His mother sat next to Anna with an empty seat on the other side of her to represent where Dorian's father would have sat. He saw many of his celebrity friends, including Darcy Walker and Julia Love-, along with many foreign dignitaries. The press had been limited to a handful of photographers and videographers, but Dorian knew there would be no shortage of them outside the chapel. A crowd of well-wishing Avingtonians had gathered outside the chapel as well.

The first notes of Mendelssohn's Wedding March sounded on the pipe organ, and everyone turned to face the back of the chapel. Emmie stepped into view and Dorian struggled to catch his breath.

She had worked with designer Elizabeth James, to create the gown, and to say it was stunning would be an affront to the word. No bride had ever looked as beautiful as his. The dress was white satin with long lace sleeves, a V-neckline and a long satin and lace train. Emmie's toffee colored hair was carefully arranged in an elaborate up-do. A simple diamond tiara from his mother's private collection adorned her head. A sheer veil with lace trim cascaded down her face. At her side, in a white tuxedo jacket, tie and matching top hat, stood Gatsby.

Emmie and Gatsby walked slowly down the aisle. Dorian's gaze locked with hers until she stood next to him. "You look amazing," he whispered, and they shared a playful smile.

After the ceremony, Dorian, Emmie, and Gatsby rode from the chapel in Avington to Dorburn castle in an ornate carriage, pulled by a team of four black Friesian horses. Onlookers and well-wishers lined the streets and waved at them as they rode by. Once at the castle, they made their way to the balcony for the traditional, formal introduction as husband and wife.

"I now present His Royal Highness Dorian Henry Sullivan Tennesley and Her Highness Emmeline Elizabeth Tennesley, Prince and Princess of Avington," the royal barker declared. The joyful crowd below them cheered.

Dorian gazed into Emmie's eyes. "You have made me believe, with all my heart, in the magic of romance when I had given up on it. I promise to kiss you and tell you how much I love you every day because I never want you to forget."

Emmie smiled, her eyes sparkling with mischief. "How about if you start now, husband?" She looked down at the crowd below and gave a wink, then grabbed the front of his topcoat and pulled him toward herself and kissed him until the rest of the world ceased to exist.

About Laura

Laura Ashwood is a USA Today Bestselling author of sweet contemporary and historical western romance, and women's fiction.

In her novels, Laura brings to life characters and relationships that will warm your heart and fill you with hope. Her stories often have themes involving redemption, forgiveness, and family.

Laura and her husband live in northeast Minnesota. In her spare time, she likes to read, cook and spend time with her husband. She is a devoted grandmother and chihuahua lover.

She is a member of American Christian Fiction Writers (ACFW) and Women's Fiction Writers of America (WFWA).

Find her on Facebook, Bookbub, Instagram, Pinterest, Twitter, and Goodreads. Go to www.lauraashwood.com to see all her books.

If you liked this book, please take a minute to leave a review for it. Authors (Laura included) really appreciate this, and it helps draw more readers to books they might like. Thank you!

Made in the USA
Monee, IL
02 September 2022